A hand-span up from the horizon, something was dimly flickering. It was in the same vicinity as the Weggismarche Obelisk—it could, in fact, have been the top of the spire—and it suggested heat lightning on a warm summer night.

Suddenly, from across the sea, it was daylight. To the south the glow was dull gray and listless, but from the north the day was full and bright. Bar-Woten could clearly see the Obelisk, a line of white drawn from the sky down, its top lost in the sheet of daylight glow.

It wasn't vertical. With clocklike slowness it was changing its angle. . . . The Obelisk was tilting. . . . and falling.

Bar-Woten was enough of a seaman to know what the fall of an object a thousand kilometers high would do to the sea and to the coastline beyond. . . .

THE LATEST SCIENCE FICTION AND FANTASY FROM DELL BOOKS

*Denotes an illustrated book

HEGIRA

GREG BEAR

A DELL BOOK

This book is dedicated to Tina

Published by
Dell Publishing Co., Inc.
1 Dag Hammarskjold Plaza
New York, New York 10017

Dell ® TM 681510, Dell Publishing Co., Inc.

ISBN: 0-440-13473-0

Printed in the United States of America
First printing—June 1979

"I had a dream, which was not all a dream.
The bright sun was extinguish'd, and the stars
Did wander darkling in the eternal space,
Rayless, and pathless, and the icy earth
Swung blind and blackening in the moonless air;
Morn came and went—and came, and brought
   no day . . ."

—*Darkness*, by Lord Byron

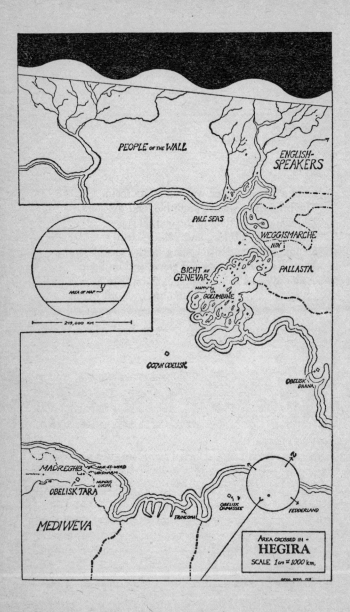

I

The Ibisian general motioned for his aides to step up to the balcony. "Look closely," he told them as they stood next to the Mediwevan deputato. "Here's a good definition for barbarism."

Below the balcony a parade of penitents was filling the rain-slicked streets.

"These are the ascetics from Monta Ignazio, General Sulay," the deputato stuttered. His teeth were chattering. He had never been closer to savages than he was now.

The methane lanterns in the room hissed.

"They whip themselves," Bar-Woten said. He was a lean, well-muscled man in his middle thirties, with one gray eye and a black patch. His nose hooked sharply.

The penitents had gathered from leagues around for the night march through Mediweva's capital, Madreghb. Men, women, and children dressed in brown sacks, black and white clerical robes, or the red of deacons and priests swung leather cats against their backs, the strands weighted to age and devotion. Beneath cloth tatters their flesh was raw as ground meat.

"This is religious inspiration!" Sulay rasped. "This is

the Heisos Kristos of Mediweva demanding they poison their bodies with infection to see His visions. Absorb this and learn from it. We've met with many peoples and their religions, but none is more amazing than this one."

Bar-Woten watched with distaste and finally turned away. His eye caught the deputato's, and he winked at the thin official. "Not to my style," he explained. "I grow faint at the sight of blood." The deputato laughed nervously, then lapsed back to his respectful attitude.

Sulay stepped away from the balcony, shaking his head and fingering his pistol's holster strap. "I'd like to visit your library now." The deputato nodded and led him away. Bar-Woten stayed behind to watch the penitents flogging themselves. Their moans bothered him like a boil under his armored vest. They were ecstatic. The ecstasy of visions. "Barthel!" he called. His servant appeared, grinning and dressed in splendid red silks.

"I think I could like living here," Barthel said, fanning his arms out. "It's cool and the clothes are beautiful."

"What can you tell me about Kristians?"

"My country had a few, Bey. But I am of the Momad persuasion myself, as you understand, and we avoid intercourse with the unfaithful. Except for yourself, sir, who shine like a light . . ."

" 'Shines,' " Bar-Woten corrected. "Your lessons in Mediwevan are slipping." He had chosen Barthel from a group of captured children fifteen years before in the now desolate land of Khem. The armies of Sulay, Bar-Woten among them, were responsible for that desolation. But Barthel showed no memory of the slaughter. He knew only those things he was required to know, and the rest seemed to sink in his memory like plum stones in a pond. He was a cheerful lad.

"Bey, I could tell you tales my mother told me, but some are very crazy. You might not believe. This Heisos Kristos—or Yesu as we knew him—is mentioned on all the Obelisks I have ever known, and his story is always the same."

"Which is food for the argument that all Obelisks have the same words engraved on them."

"Certainly. I believe that is part of Momad's divine doctrine, as his word is mentioned on all, the faithful must acknowledge that, and—"

"Why do they beat themselves for this Heisos?"

"It gives them strength to deny the attractions of the world, Bey. By punishing themselves they hope to distract their attentions from Hegira and focus them on Paradise, or Heaven, which is what their Yesu—surely a great prophet—desired and preached them to do."

"But Yesu never lived on Hegira."

"No. It is dogma that no person mentioned on the Obelisks ever lived on Hegira. They were the Firstborn, Bey."

Bar-Woten nodded and stared up into the night. Soon an orange fire dove would rise like a distant flare, signaling the ninth hour of dark, and the sky would begin to turn purple. In a half hour it would be morning blue. The streets would be empty of pedestrians as Mediwevan law had decreed for five hundred years. The wagons and steam vehicles would travel from the fields and lakefronts, and the capital would come alive with day-life: markets and buyers, bookdealers and street historians, all wholesome ser-

vices for a fee. Bar-Woten enjoyed this city and its pe-
culiarities. He even felt a mixed affection for the
crazy penitents.

"I can tell you very little about Yesu, Bey," Barthel
said to indicate he had not been dismissed. Bar-
Woten waved his hand, and the boy vanished with a
rustle of robes.

He was glad not enough of Sulay's armies was left
to destroy Mediweva. In their twenty-year March the
armies had dwindled from two million to ten thousand. They could still rely on their reputation to
achieve diplomatic victories, and on occasion a few
hills topped by lines of the remaining soldiers could
persuade reluctant leaders, but the March was over.

They had crossed fifty thousand kilometers, the regions of five Obelisks, and yet spanned only twenty-
three degrees of Hegira's curve. The survivors of Sulay's March knew the immensity of Hegira as no
others had known before them. For two years now,
since the last of their geographers and geometers had
finished their reports, Bar-Woten had marched in fear
not of man—he had killed at least two thousand men,
and they did not haunt him—but of the world on
which he lived.

That evening Sulay called Bar-Woten to the library.
The Ibisian left Barthel in their quarters and walked
down the cool stone hallways of the capital palace,
looking up at the frescoes crumbling in the dimly lit
vaults. The sense of age oppressed him tonight. So
many years, so much time to do evil things . . .
layers and layers of human pressure bearing down on
the individual like miles of rock.

The frescoes showed scenes of war taken from Obelisk texts. Bar-Woten felt the painter's lack of experience, acutely, with a mix of pride and revulsion at his ability to critique. Shaking his head and grimacing, he entered the door to the library.

The smell of paper and ink and old bindings was heavy in the barely moving air. The oxygen seemed to have been sucked out by years of rotting pulp. He restrained an impulse to choke. A middle-aged, balding librarian guided him through long, winding stacks and stopped, pointing with a knobby finger inkstained and calloused on the first knuckle.

Sulay was sitting on a stool, a large book spread across his lap. His gray hair and bald spot shone in the bank of oil lamps set beside him. Bar-Woten noted the pump-action fire extinguisher hung on the fixture.

"Young Bear-killer," Sulay said, looking up. Bar-Woten bowed slightly.

"The general needs his rest," he said solicitously.

Sulay ignored him. "They've gone a little higher than we have," he said, thumbing the pages. "Better balloons, I imagine. More texts, more advances, but they haven't seen fit to utilize their new knowledge, not yet. Many odd things as the texts go higher." Sulay closed the book carefully and placed it on a small folding table. "I could spend my whole life in libraries. Much less exciting than the March, eh?"

Bar-Woten nodded. Sulay's demeanor changed considerably when he was among books. Bar-Woten wasn't sure he approved, though something in himself was attracted to the books. "Less strenuous at least," he said.

"These people know us as soldiers, murderers, plunderers," Sulay said. "No doubt we've done enough of that. But they will never appreciate us as scholars. Yet what we could tell them! They know very little of Hegira, but a great deal of the Obelisks. I know very little of the Obelisks . . . and I wish I knew more. But . . ." He sighed. "My time is at an end, Bearkiller."

Bar-Woten respected the old man's lengthy silence. At last Sulay lifted his head, and there were tears on his cheeks. "Never enough time. Never enough. The March is over. They aren't very good at fighting here in Mediweva, but they far outnumber us, and our ruses aren't working any more. My audiences with the Holy Pontiff have been more and more strained. An old soldier's instincts warn me. . . . He will swat us like a buzzing wasp. Our reputation travels before us, even in the insular countries. We have not been very circumspect." Sulay looked Bar-Woten steadily in the eye. The old general's pupils were large, absorbing. "You will go on."

"Not without you, General."

"Without me, without your fellow soldiers, however you must. You'll finish the March. We didn't journey to kill and loot, but try telling that to an army of Ibisians. The best soldiers one could hope for, but . . ." Sulay put his hand on the book. "That's my commission to you. If anyone will survive, you will. Go now, or very soon."

Bar-Woten nodded.

"Go and find what I wanted to find."

"Yes, General."

"You would do that even if I didn't tell you, wouldn't you?"

"Yes."

Sulay picked up the book again and opened it.

"It isn't safe here, General," Bar-Woten said. "They can come from both directions and pen you in."

Sulay didn't react.

"General?"

The old man made a gesture with his hand dismissing Bar-Woten. He turned and walked through the stacks, fists clenched.

The morning of their ninth day in Madreghb brought clouded skies and a pale drizzle, which turned the capital into a fairy-tale province. The richly carved walls of the Duomo and the Middle Sacristy attracted Bar-Woten and dazzled Barthel as they walked alone through the city. Wearing his dress whites and a windbreaker, and according Barthel the same privilege, he ignored the wet and studied the architecture.

The courtyard of learned debate drew him like sugar draws an ant. Here scholars, readers, and Obelisk students gathered with their practical counterparts—engineers, geometers, and theologicans. They debated loudly over a narrow roadway that separated their bleachers, below an aqueduct carrying water from the southern branch of the Ub. Cars and trucks hissed between them irregularly. The white drizzle beaded and dripped from the debaters' black leather cloaks, pooling on the wooden planks which ran the length of the stone seats.

Barthel was amused. "They discuss the teachings of Yesu," he whispered in an aside to Bar-Woten. He nodded and listened more closely. They stood on a walkway bridge mounted on one side of the aqueduct. Water rushed to its appointments behind them, splattered with occasional raindrops.

One theologican maintained his dignity and calm
amidst the ruckus. He commanded a fine voice and
his wit was incisive. They listened for a while, then
moved on. Bar-Woten frowned as they left the aqueduct. Had Heisos, or Yesu, been a firm warrior with
words or a debater of pedantries?

The weather worsened. Lunching in a smoky
wooden parlor-house with glass windows slacked by
age, they watched the drizzle thicken into rain, much
as the grease of a lamb congealed on their plates. "I
change my mind about the cold; it is unpleasant,"
Barthel said, drawing his jacket collar tight around his
ears. "I often wish the Bey had chosen to reside in
Khem, where it is usually warm." Bar-Woten nodded.

The day would soon collapse into dark. He didn't
enjoy the thought of walking after dark to the capital
square and the Nocturne, essentially unarmed. It was
unhealthy.

They set out just before the dimming began. At this
season the days were ten hours long and the nights
fourteen. The weather promised to be foul in the
dark. The wind nipped and curled around their backs,
making their eyes sting. Cats scampered in a wet tide
from one alley into another, yowling miserably. Bar-
Woten saw why as they passed the alley—a rain gutter
edging the roof of the inn had broken, turning a dry
corner into the base of a cascade.

"It would be good to take shelter," Barthel said
from under his jacket. The boy's eyebrows, bushy at
the best of times, were now knitted to form a solid
ragged streak across his brow. His dark brown eyes
were slitted against the raindrops.

Bar-Woten shielded his good eye and looked at the
entrance to the hostel. He knew instinctively it would

be a vermin paradise. But he distrusted wet weather in strange countries. Enough diseases had plagued him in similar conditions to make him wary.

"Wait," Barthel said, peering back into the alley where the cats had lodged. The cascade had subsided to a trickle. Something was moving at the back. It was shapeless, larger than a man. Barthel stepped backward and Bar-Woten's neck hair rose.

He wiped his eye with the knuckle of his thumb and saw the shape was nothing monstrous after all. A man was struggling under a pile of wet papers and rags, weak and unpromising labor at best. The Ibisian's first thought was to leave well enough alone—this possible plague victim was no friend to a visitor without immunity. But he recognized the motions from long experience in battle. The man was not sick with plague, he was weak from blood loss. They approached him cautiously. Bar-Woten crouched next to the pile.

The man was a penitent. His whip was still hooked to his belt, lashes tangled in his scraped and bruised legs. But this young fellow was no priest or professional ascetic. He was barely twenty and nearly dead. His back wounds had festered enough to give him prokaryotic visions sufficient for a lifetime. Now he was unconscious. Bar-Woten called for Barthel to help and together they picked him up by the arms and legs. "We'll take him to the hostel," he said.

"He's in bad shape," Barthel said. "He'll die soon anyway."

The hostel desk was unstaffed. The interior of the building was fitfully lighted by gas lamps. Disintegrating wallpaper crept up the walls, and the floor creaked suspiciously. A smell of wet, decaying wood mixed with the animal smell of the hostel's patrons. It was a miserable place for anyone to die in. Therefore, Bar-Woten told himself, the young man would not die.

He rang a verdigris-crusted bell. The half-sotted proprietor appeared shortly after. He took their names and their money and raised a hairless, worm-white eyebrow at the penitent. "Can you get a physician?" Bar-Woten asked.

"No," the proprietor said, heading back to his room. "If he dies, you'll have to move him."

"I am an Ibisian," Bar-Woten said softly. "If this man dies here, I will have this building condemned."

The proprietor stopped and turned to reexamine him. "You can find a doctor a block down. He'll bind your companion and cleanse his wounds. But we have nothing to do with penitents. They aren't too popular here."

"And Ibisians?" Bar-Woten asked testily.

"Unarmed Ibisians are only human," the proprietor said. "I employ bullboys like every other innkeeper on this strip. They carry rifles and crossguns. Do you?" He turned and waddled off.

Bar-Woten picked up the key from the desk and told Barthel to summon the physician. He hoisted the penitent from the floor and swung him over his shoulder.

The stairs were steep and in bad repair. The room was abominable. An open skylight admitted rain until he tied a dirty blanket over it. The beds were in fair repair and looked clean. Perhaps health regulations were enforced with regard to beds, but cleaning facilities were minimal, toilets were one to a floor and public, and other regulations ended at the edge of the mattress. Paper scraps and dirt littered the torn patch-work carpet.

The penitent sighed and rolled over on the bed, then groaned. Bar-Woten stripped off his bloody clothes and took the basin down the hall to clean it and fill it with water. The plumbing banged hideously in the narrow washroom. When he came back the man was sitting up against the headboard and staring feverishly into empty space. Using a handful of powdered soap and paper towels, Bar-Woten began to scrub him down. Few of the wounds were deeply infected. Still he knew an antiseptic and clean bandages would have to be applied, or blood poisoning would set in. He had seen small wounds fester into deadly foul pockets many times on the March.

Barthel returned with a small, seam-faced doctor a half hour later. The man said his name was Luigi, examined the penitent quickly, and expressed his reluctance to treat him. "He's one of God's own," he said. "God will take care of him."

"You will take care of him, or he'll die," said Bar-Woten. "You wouldn't want to be charged with malpractice, would you? I can charge that against you with a deputato if you wish."

The little doctor shrugged and set his bag down. "You cleaned him?" he asked. Bar-Woten nodded. "I'll have to do it over again," the doctor complained. "He's whipped himself into a fine fever."

An hour later the penitent was bandaged and sleeping fitfully. "He'll be weak for a day, maybe longer. Why do you want to help a penitent? Did he ask for help?"

Bar-Woten didn't answer. Barthel thanked the doctor and paid him a gold piece. They sat in silence and fell asleep before morning.

Bar-Woten stood by the skylight on a rickety stool, lifting the stained blanket and peering out across the smoke-tracked, foggy rooftops at the wan morning light. The slate and tile roofs glistened with an oily sheen of dew and reflected the golden zenith. The horizon was still deep blue. The zenith light expanded and turned yellowish, then green. In a wink the green accomplished its magical transformation into blue. A steam cart hissed and rattled in an alley below.

"Won't the master Sulay miss us, Bey?" Barthel asked sleepily from his blanket on the floor.

"Not for a while," Bar-Woten answered. He turned to look at the man on the bed. His breathing was light and regular. His pale face had taken on a better color during the night. He looked almost healthy.

Bar-Woten checked his pulse and pinched his fingernails, and still the man slept. Barthel said pounding rocks together wouldn't wake a healing man before his body was ready.

"You told me your mother knew stories about Kristians," Bar-Woten said. "Do you remember any of them?"

For the briefest of moments the boy's face clouded and his eyes narrowed. Then it was clear again and he smiled. "Not too well, Bey. Mostly derogatory stories about their customs, which I am no longer qualified to criticize since I share them with you very often. The eating of unclean foods, the drinking of wine and other forbidden beverages."

"Nothing about why a man would drive himself to illness to meet his god?"

"No, Bey."

It was perhaps the same reason two million men had once left the beautiful land of Ibis to cross the Atlasade range into Barthel's land, Khem. Or why they had tortured themselves by crossing the Pais Vermagne, a thousand kilometers of swamp and pestilence and deadly reptiles, instead of taking an easier route—all to investigate legends in Khem of the City of the First-born. They had found a monotonous grassland and a central range of hills as barren and dusty as the deserts west of Ibis. No treasure, no fabled city.

The penitent was also searching for treasure, and his trek was just as rugged. Bar-Woten questioned his own sanity in feeling sympathy, but he did. Sympathy and warmth. Welcome, fellow traveler. How many souls have you killed inside yourself trying to find the right one to present to God, saying, Look—pure!

Surely not as many souls as I have killed, he thought, mostly in the bodies of others.

"Hello," the penitent said. Bar-Woten started from his reverie and looked at the man sternly. The pale face returned the stare like a statue. The lips were fever-cracked, and the nostrils were red with broken vessels. "You've put me up for the night?"

"Nothing honorable," Bar-Woten said. "You nearly killed yourself. Most people's gods resent suicide."

"Where am I?"

"A hostel."

"I have to leave." The penitent's eyes were watery green, filled with enormous black pupils. The corners of his mouth were turned up perpetually, and his eyes crinkled at their edges as though, like a mischievous child, he might laugh at any moment. But these were betrayals of his body. He was perfectly serious.

"Nobody's holding you. You should get your strength back though. Eat some food."

"I'm on a fast."

"For how long? Until you starve?"

"I'm starving now. It brings me closer to my goal."

"And what is your goal?"

"To live in the light of God, not the mud of the world."

"What's your name?"

"Jacome. Yours?"

"Bar-Woten."

"A peculiar name."

"I'm an Ibisian. I picked the name up when I killed a bear fifteen years ago. He clawed out an eye before he died. Bear-killer, One-eyed. Bar-Woten. Why do you call yourself Jacome? That's not your name. Am I right that penitents, if they try to deny the world, must deny themselves? Change their names?"

"Yes," Jacome said. "Fools of God. Buffoons."

"Then what was your name before you changed?"

"You'd have to ask the fellow I was. I can't answer." Bar-Woten motioned for Barthel to leave.

"Tell me about your god," he said.

"You're interested?"

"I am."

Barthel sat outside and leaned against the wall. His eyes surveyed the ceiling, searching for bugs to amuse him, certainly not interested by the drivel being spoken inside. He did not understand his master at times. It was often hard to like Bar-Woten. He was kind, but he loved nothing. Barthel, on the other hand, wished to love everything. But it was impossible with Bar-Woten constantly calling for him. The man's gloom was sometimes appalling.

Bar-Woten interrupted Jacome's discourse long enough to debate a few points of logic. "This Heisos, also known as Yesu, is on every Obelisk across Hegira, right?"

"He is."

"Then why isn't everyone converted by seeing His truth?"

"Because there are words on the Obelisks which contradict what he taught. Inspired by the adversary."

"How do we know which to choose, which is right?"

"By the heart, the way it beats to the right words."

"Did Heisos live on Hegira?"

"No."

"Then was his mission intended for the Secondborn?"

"For all humanity."

Barthel paced in the hallway, bent to listen at the door, then had an inspiration. He would go out for food. But he had very little of the Bey's money with him. He knocked cautiously. No answer. They were still talking. He feared the penitent might convert the Bey. A dreadful thing. He knocked again. Bar-Woten opened the door.

"Master, shall I buy food for all of us?"

The Bey looked at him intensely through his single eye, then reached into his jacket pocket for a coin. "Good food, fresh, and a variety of it. Enough to last all of us for a day or so."

Barthel grinned and ran off.

Bar-Woten shut the door and asked Jacome another question. "What made you find the grace of Kristos?"

"The guidance of my heart."

"Can you remember what made you follow your heart?"

Jacome nearly allowed a scowl to form. It sat behind his face like a boar behind a rock. "It's only important that I found the truth in time."

"But you forget what happened. Was it someone who helped you?"

"I haven't forgotten. No, no one helped me at first. But when I joined the Franciscans, they helped me."

"I want to know what converted you. Perhaps I can find something like it in myself."

Barthel found his idea less attractive when he was on the street. He couldn't retrace the route he had taken to find the doctor—there were no food stalls that close. And the Bey's presence, at any rate, was always reassuring. Now alone in a city he did not know well, he felt his pulse rise and his eyes widen. The people did not look harmful. Still, any city held thieves, cutthroats, pickpockets. Monsters to suck a poor Momadan dry. The Bey's teachings from Barthel's youth could not eradicate this fear.

But Barthel was no innocent in foreign lands. He had been raised in them. As he walked, swaggering slightly and looking from side to side to show his confidence, he thought of the comforts of Khem and how they had passed in such an inconceivably short time. The Bey had never bothered to explain or excuse the actions of Sulay in Khem—and for this Barthel was thankful. He didn't think he could stand the propaganda other servants told him they were regaled with. Bar-Woten was a good master.

But if it ever came to light who had killed his father and mother and two sisters . . . Barthel's swagger stiffened. He didn't know what he would do. He was young and no fighter. At times he wished he could be a fighter and kill Sulay, cold fishy Sulay, who cared only for kilometers crossed and confirmations of the greatness of Sulay.

But food was the order of the moment. He found a clean-looking stall which purveyed crullers, tins of coffee, and fresh vegetables. He didn't bother with the meat. Ibisians, like Momadans on Hegira, were not meat-eaters for the most part. They ate only vegetables, fruits, and fish or fowl.

He bargained rapidly and without mercy. The stall's owner, a man four times Barthel's age, smiled and gave in a little. Eventually a price was reached and they hooked thumbs.

The parcels were heavy, and Barthel decided to rent a cart. He hailed a bicycle-drawn taxi when he saw no carts were available. The hack was little older than he was and regarded him with sharp dark eyes and taut lips. The fare hardly seemed worth pulling. But the hack mounted his wooden bike and pedaled without strain up and down the flat-cobbled dips and gutters. Barthel relaxed his guard to look at the surroundings more leisurely. It didn't seem a bad city. Busy people were everywhere, and few were lame or crippled or ill-looking. It confirmed his liking for Mediweva's capital.

The Bey was still talking with the penitent. The young man was sweating and looked upset when Barthel entered. His hand motions were jagged, and he stammered. The Bey was as firm and persistent as ever. Barthel dropped the packages in a corner and sat down to listen.

"I can't tell you how I saw the wisdom of the Lord Heisos. It's a private matter."

"Can there be any private matters between two souls striving for salvation?"

"For this soul there is. You may confess what you wish."

"Fra Jacome, I have learned much from you. Would you care to raise your health for God's work by joining us in breaking fast?"

"You sound pious, Fra Bar-Woten. I know you're not. You're humoring me."

"I am sincere. I wish you to join us in our meal."

"You know I can't eat until the Fast of Francis is over."

Barthel disapproved of what the Bey was doing. He was baiting the penitent, drawing him onto limbs and cutting them out from under. The Bey had a deadly way of finding out how other people thought, like dissection. Barthel allowed himself a moment of judgment on his master.

"Your health will break and you'll die."

"Why are you interested in my health? Your people would sooner destroy us than spit on us!"

Bar-Woten shrugged and lifted his eyebrow. "I can't speak for other Ibisians. Perhaps they do. Me, I wish to know what makes a man whip himself in the name of a God Who is kind."

"My God is not kind!" Jacome bellowed. "He takes away cruelly and has no mercy for those who do not know and perform his wishes!"

Barthel cringed in surprise. The Bey had found the weak point he wanted.

"Then how did you come to love Him? Out of fear?"

The penitent tried to speak, but stammered into silence. His eyes were bright with tears and anger. "You p-p-pry," he managed to stutter. "You t-twist my tongue like a serpent."

"I am curious," Bar-Woten said. "And concerned."

"I saw the light of God in the middle of an agony so great I couldn't stand it. I grieved so deeply I died. And when I was reborn, I was the child you see now, still not mature in God's eyes. I was a scrittori. I recorded the writings on the Obelisk. And I was going to marry a woman of my own age in a village near Obelisk Tara. We were nine months betrothed." He paused and caught his breath, his wild look abating.

"She had been born the same day as a boy in Castoreto. They came from different families, but they looked alike. Some said they were twins by God's will. This boy was an apprentice scrittori. I knew him from our schooling. He fell from the side of the Obelisk and died, and that same day my only life and love froze hard as a block of ice. Her skin became a mirror. Nothing could turn her back. That is what killed me— a touch from God's finger told me not to adore the beauties of the world!"

It was Bar-Woten's turn to be astonished. Speechless, he stepped away from the bed and walked to the skylight. "Doppelgangers, I think," he mused softly. Barthel cocked his head. "Do you remember the story?" the Bey asked him.

He nodded, a little shiver going up his back.

Jacome sat in bed with his face frozen, staring stonily at the opposite wall. One finger tapped on the counterpane. He seemed willing to sit that way forever.

Bar-Woten ate a quick breakfast and Barthel joined him on the floor, eating ravenously. His master kept no eye on the penitent, so Barthel observed him closely.

"What does it mean to you?" Jacome finally asked.

"It's an old story," Bar-Woten answered around a bite of melon. "A fable. The Princess and the Poor Man."

"It's no story. It happened."

"I don't doubt that," Bar-Woten said, turning around on his hindquarters to face the bed. "What was your name then?"

"Kiril."

"And you felt God was punishing you."

"She was all I loved."

"It's ridiculous to believe God would punish someone else for your own wrongdoings. That's ego, not Kristianity."

"I know that." Jacome-Kiril was turning red, flushing like an embarrassed child. "Why did you pull me out of hiding?"

"I don't know," Bar-Woten said.

"I can't go back."

"You've never heard the story of the Princess and the Poor Man?"

"No. I never enjoyed children's stories."

"I doubt it even exists in Mediweva, or someone would have pointed it out to you long ago. It's about a man who wins a contest for the heart of a great king's daughter. The day before their wedding she's transformed into a silver statue hard as diamond. The king searches the land for the responsible sorcerer, but never finds him. Instead he learns a peasant family had a son born the same day as his daughter. They resembled each other so much they could have been twins. The boy had died at the same moment of his daughter's affliction. The Poor Man was stricken with grief. That's familiar to you more than you'd like it to be, I'm sure."

"I don't believe you."

"You might find the end interesting. A seeress tells the Poor Man who won the contest that he must travel very far to have his bride-to-be—to the Land Where Night Is a River. He will find the Princess's male doppelganger, or double, when he crosses over that empty river to the land beyond. When he returns the double to the king's land, the Princess will be restored. He does as he is told, and she comes back to life."

Kiril stared at Bar-Woten. The pain in his expression was too much for Barthel. He turned his eyes away.

"First you pull me out of my cave, and now you tell me there's some way to bring back my most precious love."

"How could I have known about your grief?" Bar-

Woten asked. "I'm no monster. Ask any Ibisian. It's a story known to all of us."

"God damn you!" Kiril spat.

Bar-Woten faced the penitent with a stare as implacable as his own. He smiled. "Barthel," he said without turning, "prepare our belongings and wrap up the rest of the food. We're leaving." Then, his smile gone, he said, "Perhaps it's an offer, a chance to regain what you've lost."

"What? Out of some fantasy?"

"That, or let your body and mind rot in a life you're not suited for. Come with us."

"You want me to travel with your army?"

"There is no army," the Ibisian said coldly. "Soon there will be no Sulay. The dirt will absorb us like the end of a river. I owe no allegiance to a dead dream. I've been looking for a reason to abandon it. I now have a reason."

Barthel was genuinely frightened. The Bey was talking nonsense, believing a mad Kristian and thinking a fairy-tale coincidence could point like a beacon! Momad save them all.

"We're both insane," Kiril said softly. "I pity you more than myself."

"Pity no one. There's no room for it. I have other reasons to make a journey, some mysteries to solve."

"What can possibly mystify a madman?"

"The world. The origin of the flesh. But mostly the world, our world. Why we are Second-born and take our truths from Obelisks." He sighed and saw that Barthel had finished packing the food and their meager burden of clothes. "Are you well enough to travel?"

"Weak. But I can walk. You compel me to follow?"

"As one madman to another. I pulled you out of one cave, now I'm obligated to watch over you."

"It wasn't much of a cave," Kiril admitted. "I haven't met your companion."

"This is Barthel, from Khem." Barthel bowed and almost dropped the sack from his shoulder. "But he won't be my servant for long. I won't make anyone follow me."

"Where does the Bey think he will go?" Barthel asked.

"To the Land Where Night Is a River," he answered, "Or at the very least, to my death."

3

"I don't think we're welcome here, Bey," Barthel said. The horse market was crowding with scowling onlookers.

Kiril swept his tattered robes over his shoulder and tightened the rope that held them together. "Something's in the wind."

"We'll stay close together," Bar-Woten said. "I think this trader wants our money more than our necks. I'll bargain. You two keep close watch." He returned to haggling with the rheumy-eyed horse dealer. The man puffed his cheeks out at Bar-Woten's offer and held up his hands. "Too cheap," he said. "These mounts are noble beasts worth twice that at least. Let's say four fifty apiece."

"Robbery," Bar-Woten said calmly. "Two fifty is all we have for horses today. We will buy elsewhere."

"Three seventy-five," the dealer said, not batting an eye.

"Too much." Bar-Woten turned and motioned for his companions to follow. The dealer ran after them, looking concerned, but a small, portly man waddled from a nearby stall and whispered in his ear. The dealer stopped and raised his bushy gray eyebrows.

"Not too much for a hunted man," he said loudly.

Bar-Woten twisted around and threw a needle stare at the trader. The man squirmed like a pinned insect, then started to back off. The crowd moved in a step at a time, grumbling and milling about.

"Knife," Bar-Woten said. Barthel quickly passed a blade under cover of their ponchos. He pressed another into Kiril's hand. "If we don't have a chance, save your skin and consider it a bad start. But go on your own," the Ibisian said. "It's your only chance, penitent."

"Is that too high a price for an Ibisian?" the trader asked contemptuously. "For a butcher?"

"For any sensible man," Bar-Woten answered, approaching him with a long stride. "Perhaps you'll lower your price with some persuasion?" The trader backed away farther. He looked at the market crowd with darting eyes and held out his hands to them—attack, now! But they did nothing, still advancing slowly.

"Hup!" Bar-Woten shouted. Barthel rushed forward and pushed the trader aside. Kiril followed at his heels. The crowd leaped as one and Bar-Woten swung his curved knife wickedly this way and that, making them flex like a sheet in the wind. Then he ran backward with comic agility, turned at the last moment, and swung onto a horse Barthel had secured for him. Kiril, unaccustomed to his own mount, had trouble controlling the animal's bucking and rearing, but was keeping the mob back. Barthel reached for the Mediwevan's reins and pulled him after as Bar-Woten cut a path through the market. The crowd was screaming and grabbing at ankles, stirrups, whatever they could reach. For their efforts they were kicked and cuffed and thrust aside by the running horses. The three broke from the marketplace and rode up an alley, stopping briefly to reconnoiter.

"Which way?" Kiril asked, out of breath and red-faced with exertion and fear.

"The east gate to the left. Farmlands and a road to the forests. The best way," Bar-Woten said. He urged his horse forward and the others followed. Behind them the market crowd surged up the alley.

There were no troops between them and the gate. In the misty morning light, bright and uniformly gray, they rode up the cobbled streets with forced equanimity. The horses pitched their heads and frothed at the bits, unaccustomed to their new riders and uncertain of the adventure.

Barthel's animal laid its ears back and tried to bite him several times. On the last attempt, just before they passed under the great stone arch, Barthel leaned forward and took an ear between his teeth. The animal bucked and kicked out, narrowly missing an old woman wobbling by in her black robes. But Barthel held on, and the horse decided to be calm.

"Farewell to Madreghb," Bar-Woten said as they rode under the gate. Kiril looked uncomfortable. Barthel surveyed the green country beyond with dark-eyed nonchalance.

"Does the Bey know where he wants to go?" he asked.

"North. We'll cross the border into Mundus Lucifa as soon as we can. Sulay's met his end, and ours will be close behind if we don't move quickly."

"Your army generated a lot of good will," Kiril said.

"Keep on your horse and watch your mouth when you're an outlaw. Honor among thieves is a virtue seldom observed—be glad I'm not often a thief and no longer an Ibisian."

"And I no longer have God on my side."

"Your journey is a noble one, penitent. You're off to save your love. We ride hard for an hour or so—hang on!"

The land outside the scattered and crumbling walls of Madreghb was fresh and fertile with spring rains. Almond trees blossomed yellow in groves on either side, and olive orchards hunkered gray-green in aging shadow. The road was a reddish-brown gash infrequently paved with flagstones and littered with ruts and puddles. Their horses splashed through at a dead run and the flanks of both mounts and riders were soon sticky with mud. Kiril bounced and growled at growing blisters. "Ride loosely, ride with the horse," Bar-Woten shouted at him, but he continued to wrap his feet under the horse's belly and soon had welts on his calves, thighs, and buttocks.

He sighed aloud when they stopped at a tumbledown farmhouse to examine a well. "My God, adventure!" Kiril rasped. "I might ask to die after another hour of that." His vision swam and he wanted to vomit.

"You'll get used to it," Barthel told him.

"You were whipping yourself only three days ago," Bar-Woten reminded him. "Which punishment do you prefer?"

The well was full, but the water was brackish. Still it was drinkable, and they watered their horses, watching carefully so they didn't bloat themselves. Bar-Woten inspected his horse. It was a dapple roan, very different from any he'd ridden in his army. He made sure the shoeing was holding up. The smithy work was rugged and durable, and no stones had worked into the hooves. He did the same for the other mounts and pronounced them fit. "Ready?" he asked.

This time they rode at an even pace. The smell of damp leather and warm horse rose to cheer Bar-Woten and made Barthel feel at home, but Kiril wrinkled his nose. By midafternoon the Mediwevan was weary but only a little nauseated. His back was still slightly infected. They found a stand of oaks and settled in for a prolonged rest.

Across the valley, no more than three or four kilometers away, a village rested in the late afternoon twilight. The white walls and red brick roads stood out in the dimming, golden light like a freshly-slaughtered steer. Bar-Woten watched it with narrowed eyes. Barthel napped, and Kiril lay on his stomach in the grass and loam, breathing fitfully.

He struggled awake an hour later and stretched painfully, pulling at the lash stripes across his shoulders. "I wish I hadn't been so thorough," he said. Bar-Woten smoked beside the small fire. Darkness was complete. The Ibisian's face glowed in the firelight, and the reflection of the pipe coals was a bead of red on his nose. "I wish I knew what I was doing here," Kiril said, "with a savage like yourself and a pagan."

"You gave up one life," Bar-Woten mused. "Not so difficult to give up another, especially one with no rewards."

"I'm a coward, I think," Kiril said. "I haven't had the conviction to stay with any sort of life."

Bar-Woten gave a noncommittal nod and put out his pipe, pointing the stem at the village after grinding the ashes into the ground. "We'll have to pick up supplies there. We have a long trip ahead—several

hundred kilometers, maybe, before we leave Mediweva."

"Less than that," Kiril said. "What happened in
Madreghb? You have any idea?"

"Sulay probably let his guard down. He was getting
too old to be vigilant all the time. No doubt he was
the last to die, though I think I see him . . . how he
died. Not bravely. The way we led our lives, few of us
will die bravely now."

"You . . . think of yourself as a savage?"

"Of course," Bar-Woten said. "Twenty years of
March and battle. How could I be anything but a savage? I haven't married a fine woman or fathered good
children, and my religion departed years ago at my
own hand. I've killed men brutally. And you're an ass
to travel with me." He grinned.

"Probably," Kiril admitted.

Barthel woke quickly and doused the embers with
urine. They gathered the horses at their tethers near a
small, grassy glade and rode into the village under
cover of darkness.

"Did you enjoy being a scrittori?" Bar-Woten asked.
Kiril nodded and said it had been the finest time of his
life.

"Did you ever wish to verify what you read?"

"No. What's written on the Obelisk is taken for
granted. Why else would God have gone to so much
trouble?"

"Sh," Barthel hushed. A group of men leading don-
keys passed them on the road, briefly flashing a lantern. No words passed between.

Most of the village was shuttered and quiet for the
night. A few shops were open still, but the hungry and

sleepy owners were grumpy at any customers. They bought food and two small pistols.

Bar-Woten decided it wasn't wise to spend the night in the village. He could almost smell the pursuers.

"When people want you dead, you always assume the worst," he said. Kiril drew his horse closer to the center of the road as they left the town. Barthel stopped, and his mount pawed the ground impatiently. Bar-Woten turned to the Khemite and also reined in his horse. In the dark, with only a few dim fire doves to light the landscape, he could barely see the road, and he couldn't tell what Barthel was thinking.

"Does the Bey wish me to follow, or does he wish me to go alone?"

"You are free to choose."

"I'm not used to that."

"You're free to come with us if you want."

"I'm no longer your servant?"

"You haven't been for a day or so, maybe longer."

"I would like to go with you then."

"Good."

Barthel brought his horse up even with theirs, and they marched abreast in the dark.

Bar-Woten was the next to call a halt. He perked his head up and listened intently. "Engines," he said. Kiril could hear nothing but insects humming. Barthel kept silent, knowing Bar-Woten's senses were sharper than his own.

"They're about a kilometer back, near the village. Steam buggies. And I think horses, too. We'll have to ride hard to reach the next hills before them." He spurred his horse, and the group galloped off. Kiril groaned aloud with each lurch. They reached the hills

and heard the clear hiss-chug of a steam buggy just as
lights appeared on the road behind them. Shadows of
horses prancing across the light-beams gave Bar-
Woten a rough idea how many were following them.
It was a large group, maybe twenty men. He looked
around desperately and saw a ravine angling away
from the road, not too deep to climb out of, but deep
enough to hide them if the horses could be kept quiet.
It pointed to a dense copse of trees where they'd have
a better chance in a fight.

"Your horse," he called back to Kiril. "To keep it
quiet, pull both its ears back gently and tug with every sound it makes—but not too hard!" They left the
road and slid into the ravine one by one, rocks and
clods rattling behind. The soft sandy bottom muffled
the pounding hooves. Water splashed and clouds of
insects rose to feather them and cling.

Trees grew above the ravine after a hundred meters
of winding run. Bar-Woten found the way ahead
blocked, brought his horse up short, and urged it to
clamber up the side of the ravine into the copse. It
hesitated and reeled but finally dug into the soft dirt
and hauled itself up the slope. Barthel and Kiril followed. A bag of supplies dropped from Kiril's horse,
and he turned instinctively to retrieve it. "No!" Barthel stage-whispered. "Leave it!"

Already the chugging and clop of hooves was
clearly audible. The pursuers were no more than a
hundred meters from where the ravine began. The
buggy wouldn't be able to follow, but the horses
could give them a dangerous chase.

Branches whipped by as they plunged through the
trees. Bar-Woten held up his hand to push them aside
and gritted his teeth at the sting. A stem slapped Kiril

across the mouth, and he felt blood on his lips, but he didn't dare stop. "This is mad," he whispered to himself, licking his lips.

Barthel's horse seemed to lose its footing. It teetered, whinnied sharply, and vanished like a ghost. Kiril shouted for Bar-Woten to stop and pulled his horse around to go back. "Hey!" he called in a harsh whisper. "Hey! What's happened?"

He couldn't see anytthing. The fire doves were nearly down now. It would be a few minutes before other bright ones would rise to replace them. He heard the shouts of approaching men and the distant chug of the idling steam buggy. But Barthel was not to be seen or heard. Kiril cursed Bar-Woten. He ground his teeth and slapped his horse's flank in frustration. The animal jumped, then stood its ground shivering and champing on its bit. "He's ridden away, damn him!"

The forest was now completely dark. Lanterns gleamed from the road, and some bobbed closer, carried by men on horseback. A bright spot came on at the back of the steam buggy, and a whining generator matched the chug, chug, hiss. The light scoured the forest, formed a blinding band on a tree over Kiril's head, passed by, then circled back on the ground. He moved his horse to one side. The upper arc of the circle passed within inches of the horse's hooves. He didn't dare speak or call out names, so he guided his horse between two oaks and dismounted. Should he grab the animal's ears to keep it quiet? He decided not to. He patted its neck and whispered to it, not audible above the wind in the trees. He held his hand up and moved his fingers to see what he could detect—nothing. The pitchy woods were full of odd sounds now that he was blind—sighs of tree limbs, leaves rustling, water groaning over rocks someplace near.

He couldn't see the lanterns from behind the tree, but he could see their backwash. He heard the voices plainly.

"Tracks! Dirt gouged up here."

"Yes, but which way? Did they double back?"

"How many are there?"

"Too many! Damned Ibisians would sooner cut a throat than eat dinner."

"Many would say one leads to the other."

"Quiet! What's that?"

Kiril listened and tried to stop his own breathing. His horse was cooperating and he felt a great affection for it. Wonderful beast!

"Nothing. Leaves."

"Don't be too sure, dammit."

"Where's Reynot?"

"He was behind me."

"Reynot, Reynot!"

"Quiet!"

The lamps came into Kiril's line of sight, and he ducked closer to the trunk. There was nothing he could do about the horse. He could see their beams dodging back and forth steadily. One lamp fell and winked out. It didn't reappear. There was little sound now but the nickering of the animals.

"Where is Hispan?" The voice creaked with fear. Somewhere a bird twittered. Again the searchlight passed through the woods. It swept over someone hugging a tree like a lizard.

Who? Kiril couldn't tell. He began to tremble uncontrollably, and sweat stung his eyes. His teeth chattered and he bit his thumb to quiet them.

"We're losing ourselves here. Back off—is that a horse?"

Kiril jumped.

"It's Reynot's horse. Somebody got him!"

"Get together in a circle until the next fire dove rises. Quickly!"

"Hispan is gone. What's that?"

"Where?"

Kiril decided the best thing would be to leave. But which way? Away from the road he might run into what had swallowed Barthel. He had no judgment for distances at all. But he decided leading his horse out would be better than waiting for the next light. He tugged at the reins and urged the animal to follow. "Not a sound!" his lips said.

His feet felt their way in the dark with tiny crunches. His back prickled—at any moment he expected a light and a bullet. But they were still talking among themselves, about twenty meters back. A dim twinkle was starting to the north—another fire dove was rising, a bright one.

"Quiet—and step this way!" he heard Barthel say. "To your left."

They were waiting for him behind a thrust of granite. Bar-Woten had a green-smeared face and was smiling like the Lotus Contemplative, without showing his teeth. They were barely visible in the dark, standing next to a streak of phosphorescent fungus.

"I've found the way out," Bar-Woten said. "Due north. No troops surrounding the forest, no one to block our way."

Kiril said he felt ashamed the soldiers of Mediweva were so incompetent. Bar-Woten laughed softly and guided him by the shoulder to a narrow natural path.

"Where did Barthel go? I saw him drop." Kiril said.

"Into a ditch," Barthel said. "Tumbled me about, put the horse on its back and spilled the supplies. But I gathered them up, pulled the horse to its side and kept it quiet until I could hear what was going on. The Bey came to tell me all was clear but to be quiet."

"Orders still stand," Bar-Woten said.

They left the forest in a few minutes and rode across fields of wild oats. When morning caught them they were riding hard for the north and the borders of Mundus Lucifa.

4

The countryside of Mediweva was slowly changing its character. Lowlands and plains gave way to high, craggy peaks and green river courses. Forests became thinner and scrubby; green turned sere, then brown. The air grew cool. And still they were pursued.

The parties trailing them had given up steam vehicles. Now the chase was mounted and on foot. Bar-Woten figured it wouldn't end with the border of Mundus Lucifa, either—Ibisians, rumored or otherwise, were not popular in any near land. So he stripped off any sign of his past twenty years and gathered together the accouterments of a mountain traveler—animal-skin clothes from the game they shot, rough bark fabric sewn together with the fibers of spear-tipped succulents, a collection of furs over his shoulder. Bàrthel put aside his Ibisian clothes and went nearly naked like an aborigine from Pashkesh—a role he could mimic well enough by simply downgrading his Arbuck tongue to grunts and slides. Kiril remained a penitent and replaced his cat with the remnants of a hide Bar-Woten had tossed aside.

The trio moved rapidly and efficiently, never so fast as to wear their horses down. They were in generally

unpopulated countryside. Replacing good mounts
would be difficult.

Because they frequently took cuts across rivers and
over fields of smoothed rock and sand, they threw off
their searchers for hours at a stretch, and thus moved
faster. The border of Mundus Lucifa grew close—a
hundred kilometers, fifty, ten. Then they crossed it—a
low barbed wire strand posted with wood and stone
markers.

As they were preparing to stop and hide for the
night Barthel's horse went lame. He examined the
beast's foreleg and found a splintered river stone had
wedged into the hoof, splitting it to the quick. Left
alone, the beast could hobble about and feed off the
grassland well enough—but it couldn't be ridden. And
it wouldn't be able to move fast enough to keep up
with them.

Their supplies were low. There was little to transfer
from horse to horse. They buried the saddle in a wadi
as the sky was graying. Rain would fall before darkness came—and the wadi would fill with water, likely
to cover their traces.

They found a pile of rocks firmly mounted against
the floods and higher than the water was likely to
rise. After checking it out for vermin, they rigged a
hidden shelter and rested, waiting for the storm to
break.

The front of rain hit with the impact of a spilled
bucket leagues wide. Rivers grew in minutes, carried
away whole landscapes as mud and scum, and rushed
into the wadi. The search party below would face serious danger of drowning unless they could find high
ground and wait out the flash.

When daylight came the land was still as death. The

grass had been pounded into a thick yellow mud. Water dripped from the rocks. No wind blew, no animals called, nothing moved.

The land dropped away ahead of them. Kiril had a dizzying premonition—where night was a river?—and looked into the canyon. It was a sheer drop of at least a kilometer to a series of declines and gorges running helter-skelter into the grandest chasm he had ever seen. It seemed to plunge forever into a murky, mist-filled shadow that complained from far away with a tinny grumble. This was the natural border of Mundus Lucifa. But Kiril had heard of a way across. They rode and walked gingerly along the canyon's rim for the rest of the day trying to spot the formation he described. Night gloomed up again, and with it came mists and fogs, which filled the canyon and wafted at the brim like a ghost ocean.

It was well into the afternoon of the next day before the vapors burned off. Then they saw what Kiril had told them to look for—a monumental rock bridge. It was at least three days away, but they could see its four arches in the distance like the doors to a Mediwevan church. Bar-Woten nodded grimly, satisfied he was seeing a true wonder. Barthel took it in stride. "Nothing of Allah surprises me," he said tersely.

Bar-Woten declared they had thrown their pursuers off. "The flood probably convinced them we weren't worth the effort. Either that or it killed them."

"Did you kill any?" Kiril asked. Barthel looked at him sharply, sensing trouble.

"No," Bar-Woten said. "I didn't. I doubt if Barthel did—he was too busy keeping his horse quiet. Did you?"

"No," Kiril said. "I'm not sure I could have."

"The Bey is ashamed that I didn't kill?" Barthel asked grudgingly.

"Not at all. It accomplishes nothing. A skillful hunter kills only for food—and we weren't in the circumstances to enjoy long pork."

Kiril trudged across the hard-baked stone and mud of the canyon edge. Barthel took his turn on the horse.

"The Ibisians must have thought differently about killing most of the time," Kiril said.

"They did," Bar-Woten said. "I did, too."

They switched, and Bar-Woten walked in silence. Birds were wheeling over the canyon, wings wide and dark. Their cries counterpointed grumbling from the chasm. To the south the white line of Obelisk Tara still gave a point of reference. It would be thousands of kilometers away before they lost sight of it, and by that time they'd have another Obelisk to follow. There would be the usual region where the sky was darker and the air cooler, then another land with its own spire. But they'd have to cross Mundus Lucifa first, and it had no Obelisk. Bar-Woten asked Kiril what he knew about Mundus Lucifa.

"There are two parts, north and south. I only know about the south. It's a monarchy, fairly backward. A series of fortresses, usually with towns inside, with high mountains and many bridges. They're friendly with Mediweva, but not too friendly. Reluctant to advance their thought. They won't allow anyone to read Obelisk texts, so any knowledge they have is from the past—over two thousand years ago—or rediscovered independently. I've only met a few, none from this far east. They're a handsome, stubborn people."

"Momad?" Barthel asked.

"No. Not Kristian, either. They worship a pantheon

not mentioned on the Obelisks—not so far as we've read, anyway."

"Well and good," Bar-Woten said. "Perhaps we can learn something from them—how much the Obelisks make us what we are. Sulay would have enjoyed the opportunity to investigate that. All the lands we passed through believed in the Obelisks. We had to make our own atlases as we traveled. No books were allowed that did not faithfully reprint the Obelisk texts or conservatively comment on what they said. And there are no maps of Hegira on the Obelisks."

"Can I see a map?" Kiril asked. "And an atlas?" He snapped his fingers. "I once read a book that mentions them. Atlas was a god—he held up Earth on his shoulders before Newton and Kopernick destroyed him."

Bar-Woten pulled a square of parchment from his shoulder bag and handed it to Kiril. "Careful with it. It may be the only surviving record of what our geometers and geographers learned. It's a map of what we saw on our March from Ibis."

Kiril unfolded it gingerly, trying to stay balanced on the horse. It was a network of lines and fields of color with shading and odd marks. He could read the names well enough—Obelisk script was universal, so people who believed in Obelisks could always read each other's alphabets—but their positions and other signs meant nothing to him. He had never bothered to read the Obelisk texts that discussed cartography— they seemed useless intellectual exercises, since no such maps existed of Hegira, and Earth was something of a myth.

"Pretty," he said. He folded it and handed it to Bar-Woten, who patiently refolded it and put it in his bag.

"There's something in the canyon," Barthel said. He pointed. It was kilometers below, a crumpled mass which at one time could have been a cylinder. The area around it was too rugged to allow easy access. It looked undisturbed.

"Two or three hundred meters long," Bar-Woten said. "Made of metal. Look how the sun glints off it. Do you know what it is?"

Kiril shook his head, no. He was frowning.

"Could be . . . like the rockets in Khem," Barthel said. "Same shape, only bigger."

"Gun powder would never lift that monster," Bar-Woten said. "It must be a building. Someone put it together and it was destroyed by a rock slide."

But Kiril saw the gouged scar that trailed behind the wreck. He had read a text on missiles and other terrestrial weapons of war—the things on which the First-born had planned to ride away from Earth. "It's a rocket of a kind," he said. He explained what he knew about them, and Bar-Woten raised his eyebrows appreciatively.

"I'd like to know who could build something like that," he said.

"Not the Lucifans." Kiril threw a small pebble into the canyon and rose from his knees. "It must have come from very far away. And it was no weapon—it didn't explode."

"That doesn't mean it wasn't a weapon. I understand the Obelisks say not all things explode by fire."

"True," Kiril agreed. "But we have yet to run into explanations for those passages. We accept by faith."

"I think someone else needs no faith. They have proof."

They were some twenty kilometers from the rock

bridge when they made camp and bedded down for the night. Dark, heavy clouds roiled above the gray mountains beyond the canyon. Rain splattered on them as they ate their dinner of dried fish and fruit, and later as they slept. When morning cast a pale orange light on their faces the air had chilled considerably, and light specks of snow drifted down. They could not see across the canyon. The river in the chasm bellowed distantly as they mounted. Barthel walked first.

They reached the rock bridge by midafternoon. Few people traveled this route, Kiril said. Commerce was carried on much farther west, where the canyon was swallowed up by a lush rain forest and the river went underground.

Like ants on a highway, the three began the trek across the bridge. The slope to either side was imperceptible, but it eventually rounded smoothly into the sheer walls. At least four holes had been scoured into the sides of the bridge to emerge near the middle. Wind whistled through them with a fierce, mournful tone. When Kiril peered into one, the draft lifted the neck of his cloak up and batted it like a sail.

"Wind and water did this," Bar-Woten said. "Hegira has to have been here for millions of years."

"Been here?" Kiril asked. "Ah, if you're going to be profound, where is here?"

"Wherever, it is not the land of the First-born. It has no stars, no sun, and no moons. Scrittori, can your learning explain that?"

"Of course not."

"That's what I'd like to explain."

Barthel said nothing, but looked down the length of the canyon into the gray shadow of the chasm. Light never reached down there. The shadows were always the same. That seemed important, but he didn't mention it.

By dark they were across the bridge. They camped again, ate, and slept until morning.

5

Kiril pondered Bar-Woten's quest as the nearest mountains of Mundus Lucifa lowered like black giants
through their clouds. Whatever the Ibisian learned,
the Obelisks wouldn't help him—that Kiril knew as
certainly as he knew he had two arms.

The Obelisks were an enigma unchanged across the
history of the Second-born. They were about a
thousand kilometers tall, a kilometer across each
side and as perfectly square as anyone could measure.
They vanished in the endless blue during the daytime
and dimly reflected the light of the fire doves at
night, rising until the eye couldn't trace them. Entire
civilizations were indelibly etched on their faces; histories and philosophies and literatures; records of the
home of the First-born called Earth. The arrangement
of the texts by subject and date was seemingly ran-
dom, but a rough progression existed—the higher one
read, the more advanced in time and technology the
records were. The highest the readers had ever gone
in Ibis had been ten kilometers, using balloons like
the readers in Mediweva and Khem.

"From each you shall choose the flavor of your
birth," the first text on each Obelisk read, "the time of

your time, the words you will speak and things you adore. All other things will be as nothing to you."

All Obelisks were the same. The civilizations of Hegira were not. That, Kiril's teachers had told him, was what the Obelisks meant. All shall choose differently from the texts, climb high or low depending on their technology, to pick what they need from the immortal needles.

They were the only things on Hegira that could be relied upon. All else—penitents, armies, generals, and servants alike—were inconsiderable. Humans twinkled brief as candles. Obelisks stayed.

"What do you want to know?" Kiril asked Bar-Woten.

"Anything concrete. I'll feast on crumbs if I have to."

"The Bey knows about its name, Hegira," Barthel said. "It refers to the flight of Momad from Mecca, among the First-born. The Qur'an tells many such wonderful tales. Not Yesu, not the Lotus Contemplative, nor any other can claim that namesake—not even, pardon my obstinance, Bey—Eloshim."

"I'd never heard of Ibis before your armies came. How far did you travel to get here?"

"Fifty thousand kilometers."

"How did you measure it?"

"The angle of the Obelisks to each other, triangulating and assuming five thousand kilometers between each Obelisk. We would pick a point on the Obelisk line and set that as our triangle apex—"

Kiril interrupted, "So you crossed how many degrees . . . say, between the Obelisk in Ibis and the Obelisk Tara?"

"You mean?"

"How many degrees would they be apart if they could make an angle?"

"Ah," Bar-Woten understood. "Twenty-three degrees."

"Did your geometers decide that Hegira was round?"

"It was round as far as they could measure. Of course there was no way of knowing if we were merely going up a gigantic hill fifty thousand kilometers across. But we couldn't see distant lands by looking at the sky, no matter where we were. So we assumed Hegira was round."

"Then there's a way of figuring out how big across it is.

"Two hundred and forty-nine thousand kilometers."

Kiril looked down at the Ibisian, his mouth working to repeat the figure. He could hardly grasp it. He sighed and shook his head. "It's imponderable. Earth was nowhere near that large. Some stars were that size. They were supposed to be the fiercest things imaginable."

"Then Hegira may be a star."

"I don't think so," Kiril said. "I didn't study the texts too heavily when I copied them, but an object the size of a star would hold us to the ground like ghosts to a funeral stone."

"Gravity."

"Even if it isn't a star, though, Hegira must be very light, or it would hold us as strongly. Perhaps it's hollow."

"And we are on the outside."

"If the Obelisks lean away from each other, that would seem to be true. And as you say, we don't see distant lands when we look at the sky."

"Perhaps Allah meant it to be imponderable," Barthel offered.

"Allah, as you say, gave us brains to think and solve," Bar-Woten said.

Another question bothered Kiril. If the armies of Ibis had discovered so many wondrous things, why did they leave a bloody swath wherever they went? He couldn't put the concepts of barbarians and scholars in one package. He opened his mouth to talk about it, then shut it grimly and stayed silent. He knew so little about the men he was traveling with. Better to keep his peace and see what they offered to tell first.

A shiver made his hands falter. "Why?" he asked himself silently. "Why have I delivered myself to wolves?" Then, glancing upward covertly, "Why have You?"

Because he loved. His love would not stop clawing the inside of his chest and burning fires beneath his brain. Move, it demanded. And he moved.

6

"It's called the Uhuru Massif," Kiril said. "There should be a few small towns and forts here, but I don't see any."

"They could be hidden along the ridges and valleys," Bar-Woten said. "I don't see any roads. No trails."

"No commerce comes this way from Mediweva. There may not be any."

"Have you ever talked with Lucifans?" the Ibisian asked.

"Not often. I was very young when we went to the western end. They don't trust Obelisk nations very much."

"They feel deprived, hm?"

Barthel countered strongly. "Perhaps they feel we are misled. There is much that is doubtful on the Obelisks."

Bar-Woten nodded and pursed his lips. "We'll probably meet any greeting parties where the two plateaus divide, in the cleft between. If you say they're not usually hostile, we shouldn't greet them with drawn weapons. But no polite society will resent our hands on the hilts."

Kiril walked beside the Ibisian's horse as they approached the cleft. A small stream trickled muddily down the middle of the wadi, but grotesque ridges and rills running parallel to it suggested this was a powerful watercourse when rains cascaded from the mountain slopes. The horses picked their way cautiously over the rugged ground. Bar-Woten kept his eyes on the pillars of scoured soft stone walling the gorge on both sides. They were near the bluff below the plateau flats when voices called out. Their owners couldn't be seen.

"*Ua hight thee?*" one asked.

Kiril frowned, trying to understand the dialect from his studies of Obelisk English. He knew the word *hight*. From that he pieced together the rest. "We are three from Mediweva," he answered. "*Trithi de Mediweva!*"

They continued climbing until they were level with the plateau. Behind a ridge of rocks ahead they could see three faces peering at them. "Your purpose!" one demanded.

"To travel through Mundus Lucifa. We are scholars."

"Your studies?"

"Folklore," Bar-Woten undertoned, looking down at his saddlebags and rearranging them nonchalantly.

"Folklore and myth!" Kiril answered.

"What would Obeliskers want with an ignorant land?"

"Natural truth," he answered, hoping to guess the correct response to the formula. They weren't dealing with simple barbarians. The border guards to Mundus Lucifa were specially trained and erudite.

"Come forward. You have papers?"

The Lucifan's command of Mediwevan was complete. He had no accent.

"No papers," Kiril said. "Our studies aren't condoned in Mediweva. We don't use the Obelisk texts."

Two sets of three horsemen galloped from both sides to ride as escort. The three behind the ridge emerged and walked to meet the strangers. The guards wore carefully beaded buskins, patchwork leather leggings, sporranlike pouches, and metal skullcaps engraved with designs in an alphabet Kiril didn't recognize. Their shirts were khaki with square, puffed pockets. Bandoliers hung from their shoulders and supported pouches and scabbards at their waists.

"You've traveled far?" the leader asked. He was a short, stocky man with a booming voice.

"Across the chasm," Kiril said, gesturing behind them. The men were tall and dark, except for their leader; almost olive-colored, their skin shining like old leather. Their eyes were white as talc with enormous blue or green pupils. All in all, Bar-Woten decided, they were as handsome a group of men as any he'd met on the March.

"Ah," the leader said, nodding his head. "Then you saw the thing at the bottom. You think we built that?"

"No," Kiril said.

The guard looked insulted, but finally grinned and shrugged his shoulders. "The Mediwevans didn't?"

"I doubt it," Kiril said, laughing.

"The old scholars drove you out of the country then, hm?" He shifted subjects without blinking.

"In a manner of speaking."

The guards whispered to each other. The six men on horseback watched the intruders silently. Kiril felt sweat forming on his back. "Listen," the leader said, "not many people come through this way, and we wonder why you do. You have an excuse, but there's trouble in your country now. So you'll be taken to the city ahead and our superiors will decide what should be done. Follow my ensigns, please." They crossed the plateau and took an old trail around an escarpment of weathered granite rock.

Each escort wore a different insignia on the ribbon that secured his skullcap. One bore a coiled snake surrounding a clutch of eggs; another a hawk with wings spread; and a third a rosette of spiked red petals. Three of the horsemen left them at the top of the ridge and rode to the west. The remaining ensigns talked among themselves as they paced, ignoring the intruders.

The Lucifan with the rosette pointed down the smoothly paved road and said, "Ubidharm." Coming around a sandy hummock covered with thorny bushes, they had their first view of a Lucifan city.

It was small but impressive. The architecture was predominantly stone, which was to be expected from the landscape. Walls three times as high as a man curved and snaked around the inner city, which rose from numerous hills like a display of stone drinking cups and hourglasses. Bar-Woten spotted an aqueduct plunging in a straight line from a snow-hatted peak. It was large enough to satisfy this town, certainly, and several more like it. The water rushed over baffles in the stone run and glistened with white foam.

Kiril had seen similar architecture years before as a child on his short journey to the western border of Mundus Lucifa. But it had been scrubby and undisciplined compared to this. The walls were painted in browns and earth greens with intricate mandalas, highlighted by hemispheres of white marble as big as a man's head. Red sandstone crenels topped the walls, capped by balls of gray granite expertly cut and polished. The city within was a complete contrast to the smoke-stained buildings of Madreghb. Brilliant white-washed masonry and plaster caught cloud-filtered, greenish mountain light and stood out like snow against the black volcanic rock. The glare was dazzling. Beyond the walls on all sides natural protrusions of stone hid Ubidharm from view of all but the highest peaks.

Barthel looked it over with gaping delight. "Some cities in Khem were like this," he told Kiril in a hushed voice. "Holy places where prophets lived."

The gates of Ubidharm were open, lightly guarded by a few men dressed like the ensigns. They passed through the outer village, a hundred-meter stretch of low mud and brick buildings dun-colored and neat, but unimpressive; then under the corbel arch of the gate. They stopped at a red brick structure, which Kiril guessed was a custom house, or a guard station, or both.

They were signaled to dismount and go into the station. The interior was square and clean with a polished slate floor and furniture made of rugged wood and rattan. The officer of the guard—without a skullcap, but wearing a green sash around his neck like a prelate—looked them over noncommittally and spoke to the escorts. He took the guard with the rosette into a separate room.

They returned a moment later, and the officer extended his right hand to Barthel, apparently starting with the darkest and working down. "Welcome to the Land of Light," he said. He was tall and black with a bristling moustache and a head shaved clean but for three closely braided stripes running from nape to crown. "Who leads this party?" He looked at Barthel expectantly. The young man stuttered and was about to point to Bar-Woten.

"No one," the Ibisian answered. "We travel as equals. We appreciate your welcome."

"I hear you are scholars of the Obelisks—readers, I take it?"

Kiril decided a modified sort of truth was best. "I'm a reader," he said. "A scrittori, actually. But we haven't come here to preach."

"No." The officer went to a heavy wooden cabinet with thin horizontal drawers and opened one. He pulled out a short stack of forms and took a reed pen from a cup on the desk. "I'll have to know your purpose in the Land of Light. Your names, where you are from—Pashkesh, am I correct?" he asked Barthel. The Khemite nodded. "And where you intend to go within the country. Few Mediwevans cross this part of the border. None for at least five years. And some—ah— Ibisians have escaped here recently. Thirty or forty in fact."

Bar-Woten nodded casually. "We heard of the final purge," he said. "Where a river runs to ground, some drops must escape."

"A particularly foul and nasty river, too." The officer's eyes examined him closely. "What were you in Mediweva, sir?"

"A balloonwright. I took my learning in Minora, outside Madreghb, and left with my companions to avoid—" he hemmed, "rigid thinking."

"We have sympathy for the Obeliskers," the officer said, scribing away at one of the forms. "No understanding, perhaps, but sympathy. We do not fear preachers here. Usually they are the ones with something to fear. The people of Ubidharm are mountainfolk, sirs, and insular, proud. Missionaries who are obnoxious pass through here rapidly. We must often apologize to their homelands."

The forms were already translated, and it took them only a few minutes to fill in the required information. The official paperwork was brief. When it was over a short oath was administered—in dialect, then in translation—and they were given cards.

"You will report to the gatehouse of each city or town you visit. There aren't many here—but if you go west you will need identification. If you plan to cross the mountains and go north you will probably have to register again—I don't know. Northern Land of Light is very different from the south. And I wouldn't recommend crossing now. It's rugged travel. We won't have you followed, but we have a good semaphore system. Any trouble and we send out troops, not always with pleasant results. We trust, though, you are honest men. Be discreet—I repeat we are insular—and please follow the basics of cleanliness. I'm sure the Pashkesher will be able to inform you what they are." Barthel nodded vigorously.

They left the gatehouse and were given their horses back. Bar-Woten saw the saddlebags had been searched. He had expected it—the map was in his shirt pocket. Perhaps they wouldn't have understood it—or, being non-Obeliskers, perhaps there were no rulings on maps and they would have. Either way he had taken no chances. He was surprised to find they'd been allowed to keep their pistols.

The city was pleasant with narrow alleys and streets

bricked and tarred, sidewalks of freshly scrubbed tile, and slatted wood window louvers painted clear, bright colors. It was so different from Madreghb as to make Bar-Woten draw a deep breath, as if he were in open country again. "You seem to know a little of the patois," he said to Kiril. "How much?"

"Very little. It was mentioned in secondary training as an offshoot of several Obelisk languages—chiefly Old French and East Midlands dialect in English. They read the Obelisks ages ago, in the Prime Epoch, but isolated themselves here later."

Bar-Woten looked impressed. "You really were a diligent scrittori, weren't you?" he said. "There's a lot you can teach us."

Kiril smiled warily as if they were jesting, but said nothing.

Southern Mundus Lucifa was barely a hundred kilometers wide, most of it mountains and high plateaus. Kiril had no idea how many cities there were, or what would be the easiest route to cross. "Maybe we should ask," he said. Bar-Woten nodded, took Kiril's mount by the reins, and led them through the gate-street.

A faint drizzle was coming down mixed with snowflakes as wide as butterflies. The greenish air between the mountains indicated night would be coming within the hour. But Bar-Woten didn't stop at the inns along the street. He seemed to be looking for something else, and his route took them through the more hidden recesses of the town.

Barthel was stonily quiet, not unhappy, but keeping a close watch on Kiril. This made the Mediwevan nervous, as though his reactions were being gauged, but without his knowing what to react to. He concentrated on the carved stonework and tile that covered the walls. It wasn't markedly different from such work in Madreghb. The predominant patterns were flowerlike, with rosettes and intricate daisy chains making the closed eye spin with sympathetic designs. Increasingly, however, the walls were the same white-wash as the upper floors, or ocher mud-brick sealed with a waxy varnish.

Bar-Woten leaned forward in his saddle and peered down the street with his single eye. The street sloped at a twenty-degree angle down to a courtyard wet with rain and slush. They were almost soaked through and Kiril was getting angry.

"Barthel?" the Ibisian asked.

"That is one, Bey," Barthel answered. Bar-Woten grunted and nodded, spurring his horse ahead.

"I'd thought they were everywhere, until I couldn't find one in Mediweva," he said. "Strange country your people keep, friend."

"One what?" Kiril asked.

Barthel smiled and pointed. The windows surrounding the courtyard were closed and painted an ageless red. A ponchoed, drowsing livery boy sat next to an open stable door from which a warm glow issued. They could smell fodder and animals. The boy sat up at their approach, rubbing his eyes and looking them over imperturbably. He greeted them and took the two horses by their reins. Bar-Woten purveyed Medi-wevan scrip, which the boy looked at closely, then accepted.

"We'll stay here tonight and relax," the Ibisian told Kiril. "I don't know what your creed says about such things, but a country without one of these is hardly civilized."

"One of what?" He looked up at the windows on the

second floor and saw a bosomy girl lean out, dark as midnight, with hair braided in circular ringlets, her teeth gleaming like lanterns between pink lips

"Oh." Kiril pulled on his horse's reins in surprise, Jerking them from the stable boy's grip. The animal reared back. "O-o-oh! One of *those*!" He wheeled the animal around trying to control it, and the courtyard filled with clopping and whinnying. The stable boy grabbed at the halter and let him dismount. "We can't rest here," Kiril said loudly. "Why should we rest here?"

Bar-Woten walked with a heavy, water-splashing tread to the large wooden door of the inn. "You may sleep with the horses if you want."

Kiril was furious. This was worse, in its own way, than finding his companions were thieves and murderers. They were whore patrons! He ran after them, but stopped at the open doorway, weaving back and forth, trying to decide whether to follow or stay outside. The cold and wet decided for him. He stood on the threshold, mouth open and moving, but saying nothing, as he saw the Ibisian and the Khemite enter an incense-filled room beyond a round doorway. Dark tapestries with suggestive designs hung in the anteroom. He didn't want to stay there. "Wait!"

Bar-Woten removed his cloak and smiled at a young woman dressed in a straight black dress. Red flower designs rimmed her sleeves and hem. He seemed to know her and to know her language, but he couldn't have known either—though communication passed easily enough between them. Barthel carried his own coat on one arm and looked around the room with the same subdued smile he'd worn earlier. Kiril joined them reluctantly, unable to say anything intelligent and afraid to make a fool of himself. But he trembled with nerves.

Bar-Woten's woman—lighter in color than the one who'd leaned over the sill in the courtyard—took him by the arm and led him up the stairs to the second floor. A second girl appeared from another room and took Barthel. None appeared for Kiril. He felt left out and relieved at the same time; but why had he been ignored? What part of the ritual had he failed to observe? His face burned, and he held his hands up to feel his forehead. He was hot, as if he'd whipped himself into a fever again.

He sat alone in the darkened room and fumed. Finally a small child—he couldn't tell if it was a boy or a girl—came up behind him and sat next to him on the bench. "*Ama sol?*" it asked. He thought that over and decided the child was asking if he wanted a room. He nodded. The child took him by the hand and led him up the stairs. For a moment he was frightened he was getting involved in something far worse than what Bar-Woten and Barthel had chosen, but he relaxed when a bare, comfortable-looking room was shown to him, empty of companionship. He thanked the child and went to the small, clean bed to sit and think.

Bar-Woten squatted in the dark with his girl beside him, listening to her snores. A fire dove's faint light came through a window high in the wall and threw a bluish square on the carpeted and pillowed floor. He ran his hand over the girl's shoulder and she hissed in her sleep. His hair rose for a moment, the reaction was so alien—to grunt or grumble but not to hiss! Then he lay back on the hard stone neck rest. His nose itched with incense. It had been a year since he'd last lain with a female. The smell of her body, as sweet (because she was a vegetarian) as that of a horse, had maddened him and he'd taken her several times, almost furiously, each time facing her calm, restrained smile with a wide single-eyed grimace.

The rain returned to patter at the window. A squabble between birds bounced back and fourth in the courtyard, spears and arrows of song.

He slept.

Barthel, in another room, kept his girl awake explaining the Faith of Prophets to her. She listened with stifled yawns and good humor until dawn, understanding nothing, then put her hand over his mouth, pushed him gently back into the mattress, and went to sleep sitting up. Her eyes closed, her body drooped ever so slightly, and her breathing became easier. Barthel watched with wide eyes, haunted and delighted, then flopped back and giggled in the dawn glow. Allah, that had been fine! Hours with *houris* were never wasted. Especially if they were so close to being Momadans anyway, that only the words differed.

Mundus Lucifa was a friendly land, if insular.

7

Snow covered the courtyard and old men in yellow jackets with loose black pants were pushing it around with brooms and shovels. Water sloshed in their wake; it was a half-hearted snow and would be melted by midday. Bar-Woten watched from the high window, standing on tiptoe on a wooden bench. Something bustled behind him, and he turned to face a parade, one child carrying a tray of food, one girl with another, Barthel with a robe wrapped around him, and Kiril dressed as if he were ready to leave.

The girl and the child exited, chattering to each other and carrying the empty trays. Barthel and Kiril sat down to the meal, and Bar-Woten kneeled beside them on a low stool. The covered ceramic bowls steamed, and hot liquid—a thick, buttery tea—piped in its valved pot. They set to eating without a word. Kiril looked between them with a fixed, accusing expression. The Ibisian finished his first bowl and wiped his mouth with a lap towel. He frowned and stared at Kiril.

"Okay," he said. "You're unhappy. What are you unhappy about?"

"Your behavior."

"You're our keeper, no? Self-appointed?"

"I don't understand why you engage in a debauch as soon as you enter a foreign land. There aren't any brothels in Mediweva, and with good reason. They're an affront to human dignity and God's law."

"Kristians generally object to love," Barthel told Bar-Woten around a bite of bread.

"Not at all! We object to the profanation of the spiritual body of the woman."

"I profaned nothing; I exchanged. I did justice by the girl—so did Barthel, I hope. You should have too. It would have cleared anxieties from your soul."

"That's barbaric! I was starting to think Ibis must have been civilized, if not Sulay's armies, but now I'm not so sure!"

"To paraphrase the Obelisks, each to his own fashion. I have been holding within for a year, Barthel as long. It does no good to hold within for such a time."

Kiril turned to the Khemite. "You're a Momadan, you should know the Prophet forbids such actions."

"Then why is Paradise equipped with such pleasures for the faithful? Momad forbade those excesses that would weaken the body and prevent his people from performing their duties on Earth."

Kiril shook his head. "It was a sin!"

"I don't understand the word," Bar-Woten said.

"You wouldn't. Not with the conscience of thousands of murders—how many rapes, how many debauches without payment?"

The Ibisian put down his lap towel and reached across with a broad, wiry hand to grab Kiril's lapels. "I grudge no one's beliefs, but no one judges for me in the name of any belief. So I am a devil. I've been told that many times. I have never stolen or raped. I have never dishonored in battle. That could not be said for all Ibisians. I may be evil, but my evil has yet to rot my standards. Understand? It may eat at me every day, but the fiber remains, and I intend to purge myself with the knowledge we find. My crimes are my own concern." He let Kiril go and cursed under his breath. "Eat, don't talk."

Kiril sat trembling and wild-eyed at the table for a long breath, then stood and walked out. Barthel looked after him sympathetically and suggested the Bey shouldn't have lost his temper.

"He's young," Bar-Woten said. "I'll apologize when he's ready to accept a reasonable apology, but I won't beg forgiveness."

Kiril ran to the end of the hall trying not to listen to the sounds that came from a few of the rooms. He walked stiffly down the stairs into the foyer, then stomped through the anteroom and stood in the slushy courtyard, trying to decide what to do. He had had enough of his own insanity.

The livery boy brought his horse out for him upon request and helped him adjust the saddle. Kiril didn't care if the others were going to be left with fewer provisions. "Let them spend their money on that instead of another debauch!" he whispered harshly to himself. The boy looked up at him with curious eyes. "*Vasheesh?*" he asked in the Pashkesh tongue—a tip?

"*Mafeesh,*" Kiril answered. "My pockets are empty."

He spurred his horse forward and left the courtyard.

Horses were crowding the crest of the road. Kiril stopped short at the bottom of the inclined street. In front of the horses stumbled a party of bloody and tattered men in white uniforms, much like what he had first seen Bar-Woten wearing. The drive was heading in his direction, right for the courtyard. The men on horseback were Mediwevan.

The purge had crossed the border. The Holy Pontiff was running his quarry to ground even in foreign fields.

Shouts arose when they spotted him. "Stop!" And a shot rang out. For a long, paralyzed moment he stood his ground, wanting to cry out that he was one of them, that he was a Mediwevan. But he knew it was crazy to face them even as an accomplice. His insanity had come to the only possible end.

He pulled his horse around and galloped back into the courtyard. "Bar-Woten!" he called. "Barthel! Mount up! They're here!"

He saw the Ibisian's face in a small window on the second floor. He disappeared. Barthel replaced him. "Bring out the other horse!" the Khemite ordered.

Kiril dismounted and stopped. How long would it take the soldiers to get to the bottom of the street with men running before them? "Kristos!" he panted. He ran to the stables, pushed the boy aside, and knocked his hand on the beam beside each stall, trying to find the other horse. It was still blanketed, but unsaddled. "The saddle!" he shouted to the boy. "The saddle!"

"*Mafeesh*," the boy answered in a falsetto, waggling his hips. "*Bastardi!*"

Kiril threw open the stall door and avoided the animal's tentative back-kick, whapping it across the nose with the flat of his hand to make it behave. He pushed it out of the stall and breathed his thanks it was still haltered. The Ibisian ran into the stables with clothes dangling and took the horse from him. Kiril spied the saddle on a rack, whipped it off with surprising strength, and tossed it on the ground beside the horse. "Is there time?" Bar-Woten asked.

"How the hell should I know?" Kiril shouted.

He walked backward from the stable trying to keep his eyes on all things at once—the saddling, the court-yard, the frightened-looking stable boy who had stepped into more trouble than he'd expected. Kiril stumbled in his crabwise gait and fell on his side and hands, scraping himself and wetting his clothes. Curs-ing, he stood up again and ran into the doorway of the brothel. Girls and old men and women were flooding the anteroom. He couldn't break through the crowd. "I have the bags!" Barthel called from the other side.

"Then come this side with them for God's sake!"

The Khemite pushed and kicked his way through. He emerged with the leather pouches and they turned to the courtyard. They were just in time to see the chained Ibisians being pushed ahead of the mounted troops. The press of the crowd in the room behind pushed the two into the courtyard like corks from a bottle. The wet stones were suddenly crowded with running, shrieking whores. The Ibisian prisoners backed off as though they'd stepped in a nest of ants. The horses of their captors reared and plunged. The archway to the courtyard was a chaos of neighing ani-mals and shouting men.

Bar-Woten rode out of the stable with his pistol in one hand. "Mount up!" he shouted to Kiril. "Get the other horse!" he told Barthel. Kiril took his offered hand, slipped on the stirrup, and nearly fell on his back, but found himself lifted bodily with great strain on his arm into the saddle, where the hard leather curve put excruciating pressure on his groin. To make it worse, Bar-Woten urged the horse forward.

The courtyard had a small gate in the rear, barely tall enough for a riderless horse. The Ibisian headed for that, and Barthel followed. Kiril swung down only too gladly to open the latch. Then, remounting and hanging over the side, he plunged with the Ibisian through the gate into an alleyway crowded with gawking Lucifans. "Aside!" Bar-Woten shouted. "Aside, damn you!"

Behind them the troops found themselves mired in stumbling, groaning prisoners and screaming women. The Grand Pimp came out briefly to see what the confusion was, gawped, and ran back to his inner office.

The alley opened onto another street paralleling the main boulevard. They turned on it and rode as fast as they could, scattering pedestrians and sidestepping carts. Kiril looked back and saw a pair of Mediwevans leap from a sidestreet and ride hard after. "They're all behind us!" he cried out. Bar-Woten shook his head angrily and turned onto another street, then around to the gate thoroughfare. "I hope that confuses them," he called back to Kiril.

Kiril looked behind. He couldn't see anyone but Barthel. The gate ahead looked calm. The custom house had two guards standing idly in front, smoking long-handled pipes and talking. They saw the riders galloping toward them and ran inside to grab weapons. But the two horses were out the gate before they could return. More soldiers mounted and followed, almost colliding with their colleagues, who had tracked the chase back to the gate after the detour.

A dirt road ran around the outside of the huts clustered below the walls. They followed it, still riding at bone-jarring speed, and rounded the first major curve of the wall. Barthel called from behind. "They're following!"

In five minutes they were on the north side of Ubidharm. Their luck was holding—a broad,well-paved road led away from the city, skirted the aqueduct, and rose into the northern mountains of the Uhuru Massif. The riders behind gave up in a few kilometers. The Mediwevans couldn't get out of the city gates—front or rear—before the chase was futile.

Bar-Woten slowed their pace after diverting them onto a dirt byroad. They dismounted next to a tumbling snow stream and walked the horses until they were calm and less heated. They watered them sparingly. Bar-Woten then let Kiril ride as he ran beside for a few kilometers.

Their prospects on the road ahead—with depleted supplies and sparse countryside—were not cheering. Barthel counted the rounds of ammunition in the pistols and the two boxes they had purchased in Mediweva. They had a little over sixty rounds and seven arrows to fit a fold-up bow that had been part of Bar-Woten's kit. "We're going to be limited," Kiril said when the count was finished.

"We won't be able to fight it out if that's a thing to worry about," Bar-Woten agreed. "But I'm a fair shot with a pistol. Yourself?"

"An amateur," Kiril said. "You were stupid to take me along. What good can I do you?"

"You'll prove your importance in time," Bar-Woten said. They mounted again.

"I'll just have to grow up a little, hm?" He said it angrily, flushing at the thought that this man would think him immature. Bar-Woten didn't answer.

The road turned from a defile into a ledge, following the circumference of a wedge-shaped peak whose cap was lost in cloud. They saw that the main road, now fifty or sixty meters below, came to an abrupt end. "Our luck is holding so far," Bar-Woten said. "Let's hope we don't run out of road this way."

8

The Ibisian fell asleep very late, shivering and half-hallucinating fires and warmth. They huddled together; their blankets kept them from freezing as night temperatures dropped below zero, but didn't keep them comfortable. Bar-Woten slipped in and out of a dream about his father and a trip to the Obelisk in Ibis. As he remembered it they had passed the lakes whose birds gave Ibis its name, vast seas and clouds of white feathers, and taken the long road through the plantations of Thosala to the spire. In the dream people crowded around the circumference of the spire and stared up. The walls of the Obelisk were covered with writing, his father told him, but as they grew closer and pushed through the crowd—which was filled with mounted Mediwevans looking for children to harass—he saw the wall was blank. "It's a sign," a tall woman near him said. "When the walls go blank it means there are no more reasons for people to exist, because there's nothing left to read."

"The books," Bar-Woten said aloud.

Kiril peered sleepily from his own mummy of blankets.

"No," the woman in the dream said. "They're blank, too. No more reason to read, no more people to read."

The crowds slowly vanished, first legs and arms and then torsos. The heads were the last to go. One head, his father, it seemed (though they were all hairless and hard to recognize), told him the words of the Obelisks still existed in their memories, and they would not be eradicated until they forgot. "No!" he said. "I'm a little boy, I don't know enough to be saved, that can't be the way it is!"

"Then why are you disappearing?" the head said. "Look, all of you is gone now."

Kiril watched the squirming Ibisian and wondered what bloody nightmares he was experiencing. No doubt they were about battles and debauchery. Then he drifted off into his own dreams. None of them slept well.

Their trackers never appeared again. For six days they journeyed across the cold passes, and on the morning of the seventh day—which Barthel said was symbolic for Kristians and Momadans—they looked over the side of the road into a broad green valley. Several kilometers below the rift extended into bluish haze, ending at the shores of the largest body of water they'd ever seen. It reached to the horizon, and between distant peaks in all directions ahead they could see its gray-blue line.

From their altitude the valley was a patchwork of farmland and unworked or dormant fields. On the shoreline a city rose. It looked as large as Madreghb.

The land reminded Bar-Woten of Ibis. Near sea level the ground was rich and fertile, and the slopes of the foothills were covered with terraced paddies and forests of camphorwood and pine. He told them of his days in Ibis—stories Barthel had never heard before—and the memories made him feel warm and mellow.

Twenty years of battle, misery, and bloodshed hadn't obscured the joy he had known as a child.

The weather was too warm and pleasant for any of them to feel gloomy. Coming through one last scattered patch of cloud onto the flats of the valley proper, they chatted cheerfully. Kiril forgot his distress in Ubidharm. It was like a bad dream he was ashamed to recount. He talked freely about his training as a scrittori. The balloons and their use along the walls of the Obelisk fascinated Bar-Woten, who asked many questions.

The road had fallen into disrepair in the mountains and was now a token trail with ruts where carts ran. Their horses were sweating and tired, so they stopped in the shade of feathery yellow-green trees near the trail for a brief rest. The wind whistling through the upper branches made Kiril drowsy, but Bar-Woten stayed alert. Barthel suggested a short nap, and Kiril agreed, but the Ibisian stood by the horses looking across the valley. He wanted to avoid more surprises.

After an hour's rest they continued along the farm sideroads until the city was little more than a kilometer away. Barthel examined the valley walls behind them. There was still that connection to make—why were some valleys unlivable to the Faithful? Because the darkness was too deep in them? Why did this valley fill with light and warmth? Others certainly didn't, no matter what season.

They made a small camp as night fell. Kiril greeted a few carriages that rolled past them on the improved roads. They were curious vehicles, orange as a darkling zenith, with glossy lacquer over wood, carved and embellished with inlaid shellwork and covered with a tapestry-like top, hung with tied leather ornaments.

The beasts pulling them were not horses, but bluish and horselike with a touch of wild moose. Bar-Woten said he had never seen animals like them. The carriages rattled past, friendly and unconcerned.

The next morning they entered the city and discovered it was named Mur-es-Werd. It was truly a city, not a walled hideaway like Ubidharm. Its commerce extended up and down the coast of the sea for thousands of kilometers. This was the heart and the blood of Mundus Lucifa, then, not the little patch of mountain communities. Kiril had never heard of Mur-es-Werd, nor of the ocean beyond, and his ignorance distressed him. Obviously his life in Mediweva had been extremely insular.

"It's that way with all Obelisk countries," Bar-Woten assured him. "When truth sits in your midst, why search elsewhere?"

"For sheer curiosity," Kiril muttered. "At least what you learn is interesting and tells you more about the Second-born."

"The Second-born don't want to know more about themselves," Barthel said.

Mur-es-Werd began as a series of vineyards and orchards. Varieties of fruit grew here, which they had never seen before. The fields gave way to scattered whitewashed villas and a central stupa topping a gathering place. These in turn gave way to suburban slums with narrow cobbled streets winding every which way like worms trailing through wood. The atmosphere was not one of cleanliness, such as Ubidharm had, but of vibrant, rapid life. At times the sanitation was deplorable, but no worse on the whole than in some Mediwevan cities.

Small rocky hills rose in the center of the city, cordoned by the crumbling walls of what must have once been an impressive bastion. A few towers, square and imposing, remained in fair condition. Around these were walled compounds adorned with Lucifan mandalas in stony green and red.

Kiril found his dialect almost useless, since what little he knew was not comparable to the northern patois. They had little trouble, however—tourists were not unknown and not unwelcome either. The shoreline was something of a resort.

By noon they had decided the neighborhoods along the beaches were more suited to them. Curious children crowded around, trying to sell trinkets and stale food.

Bar-Woten stopped at a sea wall that backed the resort beaches. He shaded his eye and looked across the bay, allowing himself a moment of awe. "The ships!" he said. "Look at the ships!"

Barthel followed the Bey's eye and felt his throat catch. They were huge, as graceful as seabirds. He had never seen any larger. He looked at Bar-Woten and knew what the next leg of their journey would be. "I don't even like water, not to swim in," Barthel said quietly. Kiril smiled, then sobered as he caught the Khemite's meaning.

"Over that?" he asked Bar-Woten, pointing at the unimaginable blue-green. The Ibisian nodded.

9

Their Mediwevan coins were welcome, but they were fast running out, and without proper tongue in a foreign land they had no way to replace their money. There was also the matter of the sea voyage, which Bar-Woten was talking up more each day. His companions tried to ignore him, but there was no way to go but across the water. North lay that way, and their way was north.

Their first step was to purchase a number of small, old dictionaries from a bookstore in Mur-es-Werd. Bar-Woten found the decrepit shop fascinating. Kiril was less than charmed. There were dozens of books lying around, which he was certain had never come from Obelisk texts—histories of Mundus Lucifa, books of maps, and biographies. It was plainly an unorthodox place.

At night, roomless, they slept on the beach. One always sat guard on a small rock above their adopted spit of sand. The waves sounded like fighting animals up and down the coast. Some were as big as two-story buildings, pouring up between offshore channels of rock and howling across the turbulent sand. At night, when the waves glowed like graceful ghosts, Barthel hid his eyes from the sight and concentrated on the light-scattered city.

Their fourth morning in Mur-es-Werd, Bar-Woten woke to the smell of smoke and saw Kiril fixing a breakfast of fish. A long pole strung with line was stuck in the sand beside him. "I bought it an hour ago," Kiril explained. "More practical than books, no?"

Bar-Woten had been learning the dialect rapidly, much faster than Barthel, and could speak to the Lucifans well enough to be understood. As he ate Kiril's breakfast he wondered out loud why the country was called Mundus Lucifa. Kiril held up his finger to show a pause while he chewed. "Simple enough," he said. "Lightning comes out of the mountains. Some of the storms are frightful." But he'd never actually seen one, other than the rainburst they'd passed through before crossing the chasm.

They made inquiries that day in the shipyards about the need for seamen. The response was discouraging—blank stares and shaking heads. There was a glut on the market. Ten men for every berth. Still, foreign ships coming in frequently had room for new men—usually because a few had been lost at sea.

"The foreign ships won't be as picky about taking on strangers," Bar-Woten said. "We might have a chance with them."

They did odd jobs around the ports, walking from one cluster of docks and yards to another. Kiril had his first taste of heavy physical labor and didn't like it. He resented the Ibisian's stoic indifference to the work.

They lived this way for three weeks. No foreign ships put into port, and no domestic ships put out. The season was difficult for trading. Soon big storms would lash the ocean into strips of wave-wracked lace. Spouts and hurricanes would begin at sea, but within sight of land, and continue unbroken for hundreds of kilometers. No, this was definitely the wrong time of year to think about putting out to sea.

There was one exception, but it was an ominous one. A large Lucifan freighter traveling on methane steam and sails put into Mur-es-Werd in poor condition. It had been at sea for two years but hadn't been damaged by storms. It had been shelled by a ship the likes of which they'd never seen, which rode by racing across the water on huge feet. The strange ship had no sails, had given off no steam, and yet had averaged ninety to a hundred kilometers an hour easily. Some speculated it wasn't a boat but a crustacean from the Pale Seas farther north than anyone had gone. The trio heard of it in pubs and restaurants. Soon it was a common story much enlarged upon.

The story changed the atmosphere around the ports radically. But Bar-Woten maintained something else was up—a simple tale of strange doings at sea couldn't account for the way Mur-es-Werd was behaving. Kiril sensed it too. "Everyone's jumpy," he said. The Ibisian nodded.

The next day brought a warm, dry wind from the southwest. The skies were colored like bloody milk. Though the wind on the ground was mild, high above it tortured and twisted the clouds into thin, smooth ribbons and shot them with desert dirt. Mur-es-Werd was covered by a pink pall, and everyone walked warily as though they were in a dangerous dream.

By evening it was clear and the winds had died. But the city was restless that night. The bars stayed open later than was normally allowed by law. Gangs of

drunken men were herded home angrily in the early
morning by women wielding cane brooms. The
women wore dark dresses with strips of white tied
around their arms. From a distance doves seemed to
flutter around the men, driving them along the streets
and swishing angrily.

Bar-Woten sat on the sand with his legs curled beneath him, watching and listening to the foamy waves.
He thought they could tell him something. But they
glowed and tossed and fussed incoherently, less pow-
erfully than usual. Suddenly they slowed to an oily
trickle, rushing along the shore with a drawing bead of
light. His neck hair prickled, and he sat up on his
knees wanting to run. It was near dawn—soon the sky
would turn green at the zenith as it always had.

But ten minutes passed and the dark remained. Two
fire doves twinkled pink and orange just above the
northern horizon. A third, bluish in color, hovered
above the western mountains.

They winked out.

Thousands were sitting awake, watching the sky as
he was. A low moan rose from the city, the sound of
distant screams and wailing. Barthel and Kiril awoke
abruptly and asked what was happening. Bar-Woten
couldn't answer. How could anyone describe something they had never seen before?

The blackness of the sky turned muddy. Not a single fire dove was to be seen. Like the opening of two
palms clasped together, the muddiness drew aside,
and a vortex of dim purple, barely visible, widened.
In a few seconds it had spread across the sky, leaving
another sort of darkness at its center.

This wasn't the warmly immediate, empty black
that had always meant night for Hegira. It was a vel-

vety dark strewn with glowing ribbons, and between and around and in these, points of light so fine no shape could be discerned. Clouds of light filled the sky. For the first time in memory of anyone living, starshine visibly brightened the land.

The city was silent under the frosty gaze of the stars. Barthel made a growling sound deep in his throat, and tears streamed down his cheeks. "Holy Allah," he said. "Blessed Allah."

Kiril's hand tightened around his cat. He felt like rolling in the sand and screaming.

The streets were soon crowded with crying, stumbling mobs. They washed onto the beaches and human waves met the water waves, forming a splashing tumult as the citizens of Mur-es-Werd tried to put out the mad fevers that caused them to see such visions.

The stars were crossed by sudden, silky ripples. Kiril's stomach sank. He felt his body crawling this way and that, yet he wasn't moving; his muscles weren't twitching. His head threatened to turn inside out, but painlessly—a dreamy sort of dizziness, disorientation. The ocean waves grew brighter, became almost turquoise. He heard a deep bass note like the buzzing of giant bees. If the whole world had been a tapestry and somebody had started flapping it to shake out the dust, perhaps this was how it would feel—he didn't know. For a time he thought he would be better off dead.

The rippling in the sky stopped, and the stars steadied. The beach was encased in silence. The people around them moved slowly; even falling they drifted like puffs of down.

Looking up, Bar-Woten thought he was going to black out. At the periphery of his eye he could see darkness close in, cutting out the stars. But the dizziness was gone, and his head seemed all right. The stars were being obscured again. At the edge of the closing circle the points of light became lines of purple, twisted, and winked out. The familiar empty black returned. One by one, flickering, the fire doves resumed their glows. The sky at zenith turned green, then purple, then bronze; the dawn was picking up where it had left off.

The display had taken about five minutes. Everyone stood where they were for perhaps five minutes more, then looked at each other, embarrassed, and returned to their homes, trying to act as if everything was normal.

But Bar-Woten knew nothing would ever be normal again. He smiled crookedly. Then he began to laugh.

10

Barthel left the beach alone before midday and took a twisting road up the city's central hill. For a few hundred meters he walked alongside a crumbling wall centuries old. Grass grew in the chinks between stones. It had become part of the ground now, just as the shell of a snail does when it is dead. The wall no longer served as armor, but as a place for people to walk by and things to grow in. From the top of the Kassarva, the fortress that circled the summit, he could look down across the town and port and think with nothing to bother him. Insects buzzed hypnotically through the dried grass and sparse flowers. A large temple was visible through the trees far below, ceramic domes glinting at each of its five corners. Inside it, too, looked like a fortress. There was a courtyard and small buildings within the courtyard arranged in a *tomoye*. Birds flew above the temple—gulls, curlews, and others he hadn't learned the names of. Some looked like hawks, but they caught fish by the sea and had red and white feathers in their crests.

He felt singularly ugly and afraid. The predawn unveiling had struck him so deeply he couldn't even find the shaft in his thoughts—where had it hit? What had it told him, that message for all to see? He didn't know. But it made him feel as tiny as the ants beneath him, carrying bits of white stuff in a line under his legs into a hole a few yards away. All these creatures— ants, birds, builders of temples—had been put here by the blessed One, who had unveiled the sky that morning.

"I am Barthel," he told the sky with tears in his eyes. "I am small. Did you do all these things that I might see them, smell them? I've done nothing in return for you, Allah. I haven't even learned from them." He asked what it was Allah wanted him to do, and Allah told him this: Survive. He nodded. He would survive. The Bey had taught him how to survive. What else then? Father and mother and family.

That was all the voice said. Be to them what they would have wished you to be.

His lips curled. He stood up from the grass and gravel and brushed his ragged pants off. "I'll also find out where your light comes from," he said. "You'll be happy to see I'm clever enough to figure that out."

Bar-Woten wandered through the closed and confused streets. Kiril followed half-heartedly, not wanting to be left alone on the beach. No shops were open, and the people who passed them were solemn and tired. The city was quiet.

"What was it?" Kiril asked after a long silence. "Have you ever seen anything like it where you've been?"

"No," Bar-Woten answered. "The sky is the same wherever you go. What we saw last night was seen everywhere, even on the other side of Hegira."

"Then what was it?"

"You tell me."

"Stars, of course. But the Second-born have no stars over their heads. That's the way it's always been."

"Do we have stars over our heads now?"

"Not that we see. But something must stop us from seeing them—a lid, a hatch. And God opened that lid last night to show us glory."

"He showed us stars. Glory is what you got out of looking at them. Myself, I had a little glory perhaps. But more important, I learned that we are not so different from the First-born. We are not cursed. It may be—" But he stopped and shook his head.

"It was beautiful," Kiril said reverently, walking beside the Ibisian. He almost felt affection for the older warrior, as if they shared something no others did. They were sharing their inner thoughts on an unprecedented act of God.

"It made my heart icy. It looked young out there."

"What do you mean?" Kiril asked.

"It wasn't all stars," he said. "There were a lot of other things out there. The fog. Maybe we didn't see a starry sky at all. Maybe we saw something else that we haven't read about yet."

They found Barthel wandering by the wharves where all the moored boats slurped idle, empty against the pier buffers. They rejoined silently and walked along the lengthy quays smelling the sea—which smelled no differently—and listening to the catcries of the seabirds. The birds sounded the same.

A five-masted steamer was at the end of a pier, three stacks poking jauntily above the steel hull. Gangs of sailors and stevedores were hauling cargo from the holds amidships and scurrying down planks, putting it in a warehouse at the side of the pier. Cranes and winches lifted the heavier crates onto dollies. It was the only ship so occupied, and it wasn't Lucifan. They had never seen its flag before nor heard the tongue the men were speaking. Bar-Woten motioned for them to follow. They boarded unnoticed, or ignored, and watched the proceedings with interest.

Bar-Woten spotted a man who stood out from the clamor, walking with deliberate speed along the dock to the passenger gangway. Khaki pantaloons ballooned from his legs, and he wore a tight blue waistcoat over a white linen shirt. He boarded as if he were long familiar with the swaying rope bridge and made his way to the forecastle, striding past the three where they leaned on the starboard railing. Bar-Woten stepped forward and addressed him in Lucifan.

"I'm busy," the man said. "What're you bothering me for?"

"We're looking for work and passage."

"Talk later." He hurried off. The Ibisian raised his eyebrow and winked at his companions. That was some sort of encouragement—not an offhand dismissal.

They inspected the ship in the meanwhile. Kiril counted their monies speculatively. "Look, with the cash from selling the horses—that and what we've earned—we can last four, five more days. Not much time."

"I know nothing about ships," Bar-Woten said, making it seem of small importance to his judgment. "Nor I," Barthel concurred hopefully.

"We'll have to eat. I'm tired of a sandy bed. Tired of carrying everything I own on my back."

"We've got a long way to go, friend. There'll be a lot more of that ahead."

"We should take any chance we get to board a ship, though," Kiril pursued. Barthel looked at him with dismay.

"No argument," Bar-woten said. "What do you think we've been planning? You're the one who's been reluctant."

"I, too," Barthel said. "The sea is an unpleasant bed, Bey."

"But I mean to say that I'd rather go to sea than live a vagrant."

"You're inconsistent. You were a vagrant on your pilgrimage. I found you in an alley. You have a sudden taste for comfort?"

"Then let's not discuss it," Kiril said, growing angry. "I was merely saying what seems best for us now."

"Certainly."

They waited until late afternoon. By then the ship was unloaded, and the sailors and dockworkers had gone to ship's mess and homes on the land, respectively.

"The captain will take a walk after his meal," Bar-Woten predicted. "We'll talk to him again when he does."

The man reappeared just before dusk. The deck was deserted except for the three and a sailor standing watch on the stern. The captain walked over and looked at them sharply. "You want passage?" he asked. They nodded. "What ships have you sailed on?"

"None," Bar-Woten said.

"You think this is University of the Sea, eh?"

"I think we can learn fast enough not to stumble."

"You been to sea before, for a long time? A year or two?"

The Ibisian shook his head.

"Then what can I use you for? Mops? Who told you I needed hands?"

No one did.

"Then what makes you think I do?"

They weren't sure he did.

"Dammit, I have to take my stock where I can! Don't think that I like your faces because I say yes. Take it that the sky spoke and no one wants to sign on! They all believe the seas will swallow them when the world ends."

"It's not going to end," Bar-Woten said.

"Of course not. But sailors are bastards for a pretty story of *ginnunga-gaps*," the captain said. "You'll report to the quartermaster tomorrow morning. We sail with the second bell. I am Captain Prekari. Conditions will be board and thirty standard thalers a month, your positions and rank to be determined according to merit and ability. Accepted?"

They nodded. The captain looked them over again and marched off muttering. Kiril turned around and looked into the filthy water lapping against the ship's side.

"Where do we spend the night?" he asked.

"On the beach. Say farewell to your sand fleas."

▐▐

The ship was called *Trident* and came from a land south of the Pale Seas. Her crew was a quiet, strong breed with few quarrels and steady loyalty. Such emotions sustained a ship over the distances she had to travel—discontent could only sink her.

Bar-Woten studiously set to learning the language they spoke, which to Kiril sounded Germanic. He had never spent much time learning the Germanic texts of the Obelisk—so far as the Mediwevans had read, they consisted of incomprehensible treatises on mechanics and a few scattered fairy tales mixed with heavy philosophy—but he knew enough to get along. Barthel had a harder time.

The *Trident* took her cargo of fiber, dried fish, and machine parts aboard a day after the three reported to the quartermaster. By the next morning they were at sea. They traveled along the coast eastward for several days, passing four inlets surrounded by cliffs several kilometers tall. Huge birds nested there, the sailors told them—albatrosses with webbed feet that could match a man's arm span. The exaggeration wasn't enough to make Bar-Woten think they were lying. Besides, now and then dark flying shapes could actually be seen, and at that distance they had to be impressively large to be spotted at all. No one lived in the fjords. Few people ever went there.

At a port called Trincoma they put off a cargo of dried fish and copra and took aboard more hemp as well as a number of unlabeled boxes. Kiril thought they might be drugs—Bar-Woten thought otherwise. "Spices," he ventured. "Did you smell the crates?" Barthel confirmed the Bey's guess by announcing they smelled like saffron—and there were several tons of it aboard.

The dark inhabitants of Mur-es-Werd had given way to light brown peoples in Trincoma with broad noses and thick lips, eyes white as bone chessmen, and tall, noble foreheads. Kiril compared his own pale skin and regular features and found himself wanting. Each day he grew more dissatisfied with himself. But he was learning the duties of a sailor rapidly enough and received few complaints.

They began their first push far from land by the end of the week. On Skeitag, the day after Geistag and the day before Duvetag in the language of the *Trident*'s crew, the ship set her sails and brought her boilers to full steam. Her triple screws churned the water below the iron stern until she was outracing the gentle wind. Sails were pulled in, and Kiril was taught the art of maintaining the methane supply in the ship.

Tanks were kept on each side of the forecastle deck that gathered rainwater when possible or served as storage for seawater desalinated by the sun in plastic tarp-slings rigged between the masts. Into this water were placed quantities of dried seaweed and dormant infusion. The tanks were capped, and man-operated pumps began to collect and store the resulting gases in a few days. The stink that sometimes escaped was regrettable—but it kept the boilers going when the wind was low and provided electricity at all times. Small chugging cylinders operated two generators for the ship's current.

Bar-Woten took instruction in the ship's mechanics. He enjoyed the challenge of the engines more than he thought he would—more than he let on he did—and soon was apprenticed to the boiler-tender and his thirty helpers.

Barthel, least literate of the three as far as the Teutans were concerned, was given standard mast-monkey duties and was contented with such exertions. Though he frequently had to crawl out on a yardarm over open, churning water, his fear of the sea diminished to a healthy respect. His skin became even more bronzed. His muscles developed into flexible and agile bulges, which he thought he might put to good advantage in other places besides the rigging. The crew of the *Trident* was integrated, male and female.

Kiril sighed at this eventuality and resigned himself to quiet regret. Bar-Woten began his inevitable romancing. For the first few weeks, however, the voyage went smoothly enough.

The work of the day was over for their watches when Kiril and Bar-Woten met on the quarterdeck to talk and relax before the evening meal. The ship would soon be midway between Obelisks, where the ocean air would be cooler and the weather less predictable. Thus far the *Trident* had avoided the seasonal storms that were plaguing parts of the coast south of them. They talked about rough storms and what they must be like, leaned over the brass railings, and looked into the water. The hazy horizon was interrupted by shadows of distant coastline.

"I sometimes think we'll forget what we're really after," Kiril said. "Or you will, at least. It isn't as immediate a goal for you."

"It's a goal," Bar-Woten said. "No need to worry about that."

"I can't even remember her face," Kiril admitted. His throat caught suddenly. "I hardly remember what it was like to hold her."

"Then tell me about her. Maybe that will help."

But Kiril found the words difficult to voice, especially before the burly Ibisian. "She was at least as tall as Barthel, perhaps a centimeter or two taller," he began. "Blonde hair as long as her waist when it wasn't tied in a bun, with a tail down to her shoulder blades. She had . . . has a soft voice. Can I still say she has?"

"I don't know," Bar-Woten said.

"Small feet. She seems so far away now. I'm not even sure I'm the same man who loved her."

"Men have gone off on more foolish journeys for less certain reasons."

"You know, hm?" Kiril said, not intending to gibe.

Bar-Woten didn't take it as one. "I know," he agreed. "What was her family like?"

"They didn't like me too much. I suppose no family likes a suitor—they bring too many changes. But I didn't fit in with their activities. She never accused me of that, or minded, but her family was very clannish, played games and sports together all the time—she had a huge family, twelve brothers and sisters. Her father was a quiet man. He managed a business in a small town called Torres de Cristobal. He owned a small ranch and raised cattle. I was a scrittori—not a very reliable occupation, not much better than being a student or a theologican. But I was doing well enough that they couldn't fault me my choice of life-times."

"Choice of lifetimes?"

"Of course. A man chooses when he is to be born, to carry out a certain task on Hegira. If he chooses wrongly, then he comes at an inopportune time, and he can only turn out bad or useless. I was doing well enough not to be useless."

"What was her name?" Bar-Woten asked.

"Elena," he said.

Barthel began taking lessons in navigation from three deck officers. He was getting better with the language, and two of his teachers could speak passable Lucifan. In turn for his lessons he offered them lessons in Arbuck, which some of the western coastal countries spoke and which had always been a mystery to the crew of the *Trident*.

Navigation on Hegira, they explained, was entirely different from navigation as described by the Obelisk texts. There were different objects to be sighted and different problems to be dealt with. The meteorology of Hegira was radically different from old Earth, and there were no stars or sun or moon to use as guides. Instead the paths of certain fire doves were charted, and each fire dove was given a name according to its peculiar qualities. In all there were at least five hundred different fire doves, two dozen of which were easily discernible. They could be identified by color and brightness, not unlike the methods used by the First-born to distinguish stars, but the fire doves were obviously not stars. They were not fixed—they wandered in relation to each other according to complex orbits, all of which centered on Hegira. Not all the orbits had been calculated, however. Only ten especially bright fire doves were used for most navigational problems.

One of the major problems of navigation was knowing when a fire dove would be illuminated. Each had its own cycle of light and dark, which ranged from seven hours to six months. It was considered bad form to be tracking a fire dove and have it unexpectedly go out on you.

During the day prevailing winds—which seldom shifted—were used to indicate direction, according to how the ship ran with them. Some ocean currents were also used as guides. When weather permitted the Obelisks were referred to, and these fixed points were the most reliable. The four points of the compass weren't used in their normal sense by Hegirans. Magnetized needles didn't point any particular direction, though it was rumored that lodestone poles did exist to the very far northwest. The side of an Obelisk that began with the invocation text was called the north side. Left of it was west, right east, and opposite, south. Beyond that one traveled by original orientation, using Obelisks and fire doves as references.

The *Trident* would soon lose sight of the Obelisk Tara in Mediweva, and of the Obelisk Onmassee east of it in the central highlands of Fedderland. Trincoma was the westernmost port of Fedderland, and while the Obelisk Onmassee was not visible from that city, ten kilometers out to sea brought it into plain view.

Barthel studied the books and charts given to him. They obviously did not come from Obelisk texts. Therefore the crew of the *Trident*, though they came from a land that had access to an Obelisk, didn't share the prejudices of the Mediwevans. He read voraciously.

One of his teachers was a deck officer named Avra, a woman at least twice Bar-Woten's age, with thick black hair and a thin, stern face. Her eyes were the same green as the phantom lights that formed rings in the waves at night. She spoke in a small, precise voice and carried her shoulders with an arrogant squareness belying her personality, which was pleasant and gracious. She was a widow. Her husband had been a methane-tender, and they had sailed on the *Trident* for twenty years together in more foreign ports and strange seas than anyone else aboard, even the captain, who had joined the ship four years before. At age fifteen she had hired on as a cook, and all her training and schooling had been aboard the *Trident*. She was an excellent teacher, and she found the Khemite an eager pupil.

Bar-Woten remained quietly puzzled by the *Trident*. She had no true home port, though most of her crew called the country of Weggismarche home. They were heading there now, by way of a few ports along the Bicht av Genevar, a broad archipelago between Weggismarche and the Obelisk Daana. In a few months they would pass the Ocean Obelisk. The *Trident* had spent most of her half-century in these waters plying trade between the islands and Weggismarche. In this way she had developed a good reputation that sustained her when she had been isolated from her previous owners through several revolutions in Weggismarche. For a few harsh years she had become a pirate of sorts.

But that was all past now. The *Trident* carried only a token complement of guns that were powerful enough for defense, but would never let her play the role of a raiding ship. Besides, she wasn't fast enough.

What puzzled the Ibisian was the spirit of cooperation that powered the ship almost as much as the wind. Survival in the tough trade of the Bicht av Genevar and elsewhere was apparently determined by blatant and dependable honesty. He had never known a system run in such a way. He doubted its efficacy.

Kiril accepted it with a joyous heart. He listened intently to stories told by the crew of dozens of encounters with civilizations that had never known foreign trade, or even foreigners—without a single mishap. "She's a goddess!" he told Bar-Woten enthusiastically, patting the varnished oak railings. "One king even called her a *Kwan-Yin*—Mercy. What a ship we chose to join!"

The Ibisian kept his silence and learned all he could about the lands the *Trident* had visited. He kept a notebook in which he drew his maps and charts and recorded private observations.

They had been at sea for three months without sight of land, navigating by the Ten Agreeable Fire Doves, when a call for general quarters was rung. The crew took positions in a few minutes. Nothing could be spotted from the decks, but the lookout in the mainmast tower-nest had spotted something odd ahead of them. Within a quarter hour people on the decks spotted it too.

Kiril was standing next to a wiry old man who usually supervised repairs to the ship's sails and deck canvas. The old sailor's eyes were sharper than Kiril's—he held his hand above them and mumbled something about it being the largest he'd ever seen.

"What is it?" Kiril asked, almost shaking. The sea was suddenly a very unpleasant place again, green and cold and unknown.

"*Untersay draken*," the canvasmaker answered.

"What's that?" Kiril wanted—and at the same time didn't want—specifics.

"*Spruten.*"

"I don't know that word."

"*Ochobras, diesbras, dolfijn-manker.*"

No better off than before, he turned his eyes back to the horizon and saw it. At first it looked like a thick tangle of what the sailors called sargass, a weed that formed in ocean eddies like floating islands. But its pulpy tendrils took on a ropey sort of life which made his neck hairs crawl. Sometimes it was pink, sometimes blue. He regretted ever leaving his landlocked home.

"*Polypus,*" another sailor said, approaching the rail to get a better view, pointing with a lean brown finger. Kiril looked at him, and the man raised his shaggy eyebrows urging him to see it while he could. "Rare sight!" he explained. "Makes a seaman of you."

"Or a pudding," another said. A few women and one young girl joined the group, and Kiril tried to pull himself together for their benefit. But he still trembled.

The *polypus*—a word close enough to the Mediwevan equivalent that he could understand they were talking about a squid—was basking without much concern off the port side, barely a hundred meters away. The *Trident* was giving it a wide berth. It was common knowledge that *untersay drakens*, like fishermen's floats, carried nine tenths of their bulk below the water line.

At night the sea was alive with glowing lights. This was truly the realm of *drakens*, Kiril learned—a hundred leagues of squid and glowing fish and *fliegen-say-drakens,* which could land on deck and squash a man, but were harmless otherwise. Then there was the possibility of meeting a pack of true serpents, not shy like the squid, not harmless like the flying beasts, but carnivorous and nasty and difficult to drive off.

Bar-Woten was unpleasantly awed as he stared over the railing and saw the lights pass and flash in the depths. Overhead were the fire doves in the velvet black sky, and below that the glowing soup of the sea's surface, and beneath that luminous spots like eyes as wide across as the spread of his arms. The night was alive with seeing things and glowing things and curious unknown things. He had never known discomfort—or even fear—like what he felt now, even on the worst and most wretched nights of the March.

But with morning the sea was blue and bright and the air was warmer. No more fleshy masses were spotted, and some cheer returned.

Barthel watched the temperature rise on the ship's thermometers as they entered the region of the Ocean Obelisk. He frowned each time he stood at the base of the mainmast, where the instruments were mounted on a mahogany plaque. He scratched his head and squinted comically. Then, when the Obelisk was in plain view, just before nightfall as the sky dimmed and turned gold and green, his frown cleared. He looked at the thermometers with astonishment and started to shout.

"It's simple!" he yelled. "It's so beautifully simple!"

12

Bar-Woten and Kiril took turns leaning on the wrench, grunting and straining in the close dark heat of the engine room bilge. The wrench was wrapped around a fist-sized nut that held a tension plate in position, keeping a secondary rod on the high-pressure cylinder in line with its swing alley. It had been rubbing for a day, causing a hideous screech with each pump and swing that echoed through the engine and made the crankshaft tremble and buck. With the gradual loosening of the nut the tension plate could be shifted by deft hammer blows until the H.P. cylinder rod crept back into line. It was rough, filthy work with paint rubbing off on their pants and sweat flooding over their cotton brow-bands and prickling in their eyes. They set the wrench and hammer down for a rest. Bar-Woten rubbed the blisters on his hand.

Feet banged down the ladder from the upper engine room catwalk. "I've figured it out!" Barthel shouted. "I've got it!"

He sat down next to them on one of the main bearings, squirming on the uneven surface, and told them. It came out in a quick and happy babble, in Medi-wevan, which most of the attending engine hands didn't understand, leaving them to sit and listen blankly on the port stringer beam and bilge keelson.

"That means the Obelisks have light and heat on top," he concluded. "That explains why some deep canyons are dark the same way all the time and others aren't."

Bar-Woten nodded, too tired to think. Kiril leaned against a condenser pipe and said it sounded convincing.

"It's very important," Barthel said, disappointed that his excitement wasn't communicating itself. He looked from face to face and tried to explain it to the other sailors in broken Teutan. They nodded agreeably. Frustrated, he stood and brushed his pants off, turned around, and looked at the engine as though he distrusted it and all other deaf and dumb things he couldn't explain himself to. He climbed out of the engine-well and went about on deck to look for Avra.

Kiril and Bar-Woten switched with another pair of sailors, and the wrenching and hammering continued.

The water became warmer and more turbulent. Great spouts tore the sea into ragged shards to the west. In a few days the water cooled slightly, but the temperature increase grew steadier the closer they approached the Ocean Obelisk.

Avra helped Barthel put his theory into writing, and together they gathered facts and figures to back it up. He was disappointed to find the idea wasn't original with him, but he still worked to prove his assertions, and Avra tutored him on how to go about the research.

The Ocean Obelisk passed on the port side the day after the engine overhaul was completed. Kiril watched it from the railing and thought about Barthel's theory, wondering how correct he was. His

world was taking shape more each day. He thought he
might have it all in the palm of his hand in a few
more years. The Obelisks were higher than the air,
and the sun did not rise or set on the Second–born,
but grew bright or dim, and perhaps hid where nothing but its light could be seen . . . He daydreamed
for an instant, and the Obelisk turned scaly and
writhed like the tail of a dragon. He shook his head
briskly to clear it. In a week the Obelisk was in the
horizon haze.

The smell of the sea changed as they approached
the waters of the Bicht. Islands grew more numerous,
some with small fishing settlements and huts on tall
poles. The sea frequently rose above the islands during a storm, Bar-Woten learned. It was a rough life.
Still people clung like barnacles, and he knew the
glue that held them was the past. Where the past had
meaning, people stayed.

The *Trident* did brisk trade between the islands,
also acting as a hauler and mediator. Her principal
load was destined for Weggismarche, but she had several tons of tools and nets which she'd picked up on
other landfalls. Kiril and Barthel helped with the in-
ventory. Bar-Woten drove one of the motor launches
that delivered the goods to the islands lacking port facilities.

In these weeks they saw white beaches backed with
palm trees that rustled and crackled in the breeze,
and high green mountains thick with brush no man
had ever crawled through, and islands so big there
was no way to tell they weren't the mainland until you
had sailed completely around one and seen the same
banyan tree from two directions. Kiril breathed it in
and blew it out and took energy from it all. At night

he ran his hands along his back and felt the ridges of lash scars there, asking: Who did this? I did? Not me. The other one.

The Young One.

He worked with the loading crews on cargo watches until sweat covered him in a fine sheen. He helped trim and refit piping from the methane tanks and went with the boats to kelp beds to gather the great underwater trees. On deck they hung in canvas-covered bags until they were cut and stacked to dry. The smell was outrageous. In a few days, though, they were in neat odorless blocks, boxed and stored for use in the methane-generation tanks. The wind was from the sea, and the kelp was from the sea, and he knew, as he sweated in the day and felt his scars by night, that the *Trident* did nothing to the sea that any other sea creature didn't do. He was no longer a penitent, a traveler out of fear, but a crewman of the *Trident*.

Conversely, Bar-Woten enjoyed the work and grew familiar with the sea, but was not part of the ship. He could never wholeheartedly join anything again. He worked with the boilers and the engine and knew them for what they were, pieces of metal that filled and pumped and thrust, not parts of a living thing.

Barthel's enthusiasm seldom reached him. Most of what the Khemite was learning from Avra wouldn't be much use to them when they landed in the north and started the trek again. It seemed to Bar-Woten that the original journey was losing steam. It was being absorbed into this lesser, niggling trip across sea and between islands.

The central island of the Bicht was called Golumbine. It was twenty-five hundred kilometers from Weggismarche. On extremely clear days, the Weggismarche Obelisk could be seen from its northern side as an almost invisible line. The *Trident* sailed around the eastern tip, passing huge pillars of granite topped with temples carved from solid rock thousands of years ago. Above the beaches, in the craggy hills, three statues rose from the jungle. Each was a hundred meters tall, made from bronze almost black with the centuries. The central sculpture was a woman dancing, her right leg crooked to put her foot just over her left knee, both arms held out with palms up toward the sky. She was rounded and stocky, built to hold her weight as much as to resemble a woman. Her hair radiated in bronze sunbursts, a fan of metal twenty meters wide. To each side her companion statues were serpents curling around central columns of rock white as snow, except where the bronze had stained them green.

The *Trident* put into the deepwater port in the north of the island eight months after leaving Mur-es-Werd, and the brown, light-haired inhabitants welcomed them to Golumbine. Liberty was granted to all aboard the ship but a skeleton watch, of which Bar-Woten was a disgruntled member.

That evening the crew of the *Trident* feasted in a palace made of quartz. It was only the climax of a heady day spent as near-heroes, welcomed after a long absence at sea by a kingdom the *Trident* had saved from starvation during droughts three years before. The crew and officers were led along the bund in the late afternoon after the day's business had been completed and seated in a shady building of white wood slats and rattan roofing. While they were served drinks in the hard rinds of *sati*, a juicy red-fleshed fruit, wagons pulled by large island deer were parked

in front. They climbed in with drinks in hand and
were driven along a path that snaked through an or-
chard, rose gently to a hilltop, and after an exhilarat-
ing downhill gallop, presented them to the stone city
of Mappu.

Mappu was at least ten thousand years old, Avra
told Kiril and Barthel as they rode in the cart. A thousand years ago it had been rebuilt because its stones
had grown too worn to be dignified. In all that time it
had known only three dynasties of royal families.
Each had succeeded without bloodshed under the de-
crees of the priests and priestesses of Dat, the goddess
whose statue rose on the island's eastern peninsula.
There had been some war with western islands during
the past two hundred years, but Golumbine was now
at peace. Its hundred-and-fifty-kilometer length supported fifty thousand people comfortably.

She finished her history just as the carts pulled up
to the crystalline palace. The officers and crew
stepped down and milled at the base of the white
marble steps. Footprints had worn grooves in the
stone. Above the steps a half-circle arch of white
quartz led to the alcove of the main hall. The arch
was covered with etched figurines engaged in every
aspect of living—farming, herding, studying, building,
eating, making love, giving birth, dying . . . corona-
tion and funerals, life and death in dizzying detail.
Barthel patiently ignored them. Kiril was less circumspect. He walked with the others into the alcove
beneath the arch, frustrated and curious to examine it
longer. They were taken into the main hall.

Curtains and banners hung rippling with red and
green ribbons tied at their ends, suspended from raf-
ters of dark rich wood inlaid with bone and ivory

friezes. Low tables covered by white cloth with a bowl at each place setting awaited them, covering the floor of the hall. The men and women and children of throne.

At one side of the hall was a curtained stage. The curtains coursed with the activity behind them, sequins twinkling in the red and green and blue silk.

Everyone stood. Whispers passed—the Queen and King were approaching. Kiril expected long, fine robes and blaring trumpets, but there was no fanfare or pomp. He could barely see the throne over the heads of his crewmates, but what he did see caught him off guard.

The Queen and King were little more than a meter high, well proportioned, and graying with age, dressed in simple gray suits and without crowns or any overt signs of distinction. They took their seats— the Queen on her throne, the King at her feet. The meal was served.

The first course was clear broth soup with bits of crunchy vegetable floating in it, spiced with curry. the *Trident* took their seats on pillows. The captain was given a seat of honor next to a simple wooden Then came a dish of wheat grains steamed and topped with a sauce of shellfish and green beans. The main course was *matu paka*, beef and pork cooked in broth and butter and garnished with thick leaves of sweet cabbage. Barthel picked at it without enthusiasm—pork was a forbidden item for him—but Kiril thought he'd never tasted anything so delicious. A grain liqueur, sweet and biting, was served with thick cream and a coffeelike brew. Dessert followed. When the company was through with the spiced fruit and cream-egg chiffon, the entertainment began.

The curtains drew aside, showing a stage empty except for voluminous folds of blue cloth draped over hidden set pieces and lighted by dozens of insect-wax lamps. A single man, also dressed in blue, rose from behind a draped box and stood on top of it, drawing a fan from his shirt and spreading it wide. He smiled, whistled, and beckoned with the fan to the left of the stage.

Some of the crew knew what to expect. Many others didn't, and a cry of dismay went up as the beast stalked onto the stage. Barthel felt a chill, as though he were seeing something ungodly.

It was about two meters tall and stood on thick, powerful hind legs, balanced by a sinuous tail. It was sky blue around its throat and stomach and dewlaps and enamel green like a beetle everywhere else. Its eyes were red as rubies and ringed with black and orange. It was a magnificent animal, its gait as smooth as a dancer's, its long mouth studded with glittering teeth. It bowed to the man in blue and hunkered down in the middle of the stage with its tail curled under it. It bird-blinked back to front with nictitating membranes as it surveyed the audience. A thick black tongue slithered between iridescent lips.

A woman in red, dressed in baggy pants and shirt much like the man, stood up and climbed onto another draped pedestal. She produced a second fan, spread it, and beckoned to the right. A man-tall, heavy-beaked bird crossed the stage and perched in front of her, beak open, staring and twisting its head. It looked more alarmed than its reptile companion. A second man summoned two lions, and a second woman brought out a tiger four meters long from head to tail with gray-green and white stripes instead

of the usual black and orange. The animals took their
positions quietly.

The first man began a gliding dance around the
stage between the animals. The tiger licked one paw
contentedly. The bird stalked forward and joined the
man in a strange, appealing ballet. The first woman
began her own dance, and the tiger stalked with per-
fect precision under her swirling legs. The reptile
stood up.

With the lions joining they became a shifting in-
and-out sequence of fluid bodies and startling colors.
The first dance ended with one woman riding the tiger and a man leading the reptile by a short halter.
Kiril couldn't break his eyes away. He expected disaster and carnivorous reprisal at any instant. As the curtains closed the crew of the *Trident* crossed their arms
and slapped their palms against their biceps. Kiril and
Barthel mimicked the applause. A grin covered the
Khemite's face, and his eyes sparkled like a child's.

The chandeliers lighting the hall tinkled and quiv-
ered slighty. Kiril felt his neck hair prickling. A low,
inaudible vibration passed through the floor and tables. The hall was suddenly quiet. Behind the curtains
the sounds of scuffling and growls interrupted the silence.

There were no quakes on Hegira. There were no
records of quakes except on the Obelisks, and it was
assumed they were plagues visited upon the First-born
in moments of hubris. But very clearly the palace
lights were swaying, and the floor sustained its sub-
sensuous murmur. The King and Queen stood up hesitantly, and a retinue of guards surrounded them. A
man dressed in flowing, shiny green robes passed
along one side of the hall with two lackeys in red fol-

lowing, each carrying bowls of incense. They left the hall.

The reptile poked through the curtains and stood on the apron of the stage, uncertain and unwilling to jump into the audience. A trainer dressed in black came out and led it backstage again. Its tail swished back and forth under the curtain like a cat's.

Barthel crouched wide-eyed by the table.

The captain ordered his crew to be seated.

Outside, it had been dark for an hour and a slight drizzle was falling. The watch on the *Trident* felt the tremor as a singing in the hull. Water rippled from the shore, and the logs of the bund creaked.

Bar-Woten walked up the ladder from the engine room and went to the port side to stare out into the dark. He could see nothing but the patient gleam of the fire doves and small, fitful glows of disturbed animals in the water. He squinted his eyes, looking directly north.

A hand span up from the horizon, something was dimly flickering, and it wasn't a fire dove. It was in the same vicinity as the Weggismarche Obelisk—could, in fact, have been the top of the spire—and it suggested heat lightning on a warm summer night. Its flicker sent sympathetic flashes across the sky like messages between gods.

Suddenly, from across the sea, it was daylight. To the south the glow was dull gray and listless, but in the north the day was full and bright. Bar-Woten saw the Obelisk clearly, a line of white drawn from the sky down, its top lost in the sheet of daylight glow.

It wasn't vertical. With clocklike slowness it was changing its angle. The tremble that made his feet ache and his head throb was a much-reduced and distant effect. The Obelisk was tilting and falling.

He was enough of a seaman now and had studied the charts enough to know that anything of such size falling would create havoc along that distant sea and coastline. The result would be more quakes, and something he had never imagined until now, but knew was inevitable.

The sea would rise from the collision of world and spire like an unleashed monster. He knew instinctively it would carry itself to Golumbine and beyond. He had no idea how fast such a vibration could travel through water or the land beneath, but it would be rapid. They had three or four hours at most to prepare.

He ran to the poop deck and told a cabin boy to take a message to the captain. As the boy ran to the gangway and crossed to the shore, the Ibisian saw the final moment of the fall.

In awful silence the spire dropped below the horizon. The daylight flickered and blinked out.

With agonizing awareness of his ignorance, Bar-Woten tried to calculate how long they had. He had learned enough about basic physics in the last few months to make a guess—it would be measured in hours instead of minutes—but how many? Sound traveled through rock faster than through air or water.

In a half hour the crew and hundreds of Golumbines were running along the bund and docks.

The captain boarded without ceremony and issued a call to general quarters. "We're taking the ship out to sea," he shouted. Sails were rigged and steam was brought up. The boilers protested the rapid heating by creaking and pounding.

In another half hour the ship was ready to cruise at one third out of the harbor. The Golumbines followed its example, hauling their boats ashore if they were small enough or following the *Trident* out to sea. Bar-Woten watched the barges and outrigged clippers following in their wake. In the wavering glow of lamps mounted along the sides of the boats, he saw the faces of sailors working at oars and rigging or simply waiting, eyes north and mouths wide.

When the engines were up to full steam he turned his deck gauge over to another sailor and went to find Kiril.

The Mediwevan was stowing gear with a dozen other men. Bar-Woten helped them, and as they worked he asked Kiril what he had read about big waves and the First-born.

"They were called tidal waves," Kiril said. "That's about all I know. But we don't have any tides here—I'm not even sure they were caused by tides on Earth." He shook his head. They'd never seen really big waves except those caused by a storm at sea, such as the waves on the beaches in Mur-es-Werd. "If the Obelisk fell—"

"It fell!" Bar-Woten said firmly.

"Then we probably won't survive."

"What are they going to do on the island?"

"Head for the highest hills they can find. Or behave like people usually do and be washed out to sea. I don't know! The captain warned them, but he doesn't know what he's talking about any more than the rest of us."

The *Trident* was four kilometers northwest of the island when the captain decided the water was deep enough. The sails were furled, and all the ship's hatches battened and bolted. The bow was swung about in the direction of the Obelisk, and the boilers were cooled. The excess methane in the tanks and fire chamber was blown out the rear through valves. All compressed gas tanks were double sealed and anchored to the deck plates and beams with thick rubber-coated chains.

It was quiet. The crew secured themselves below decks to stanchions and bulkhead hooks, using slip-knots in case they had to abandon ship. The *Trident* made her usual share of ship noises. The water lapped against her steel hull.

An hour and a half after the fall the distant island hummed and wailed like a bottled demon. The deck watch and the captain and officers in the bridge observed through binoculars. Trees cast off their leaves like dogs shivering water.

From the north they could hear a wind rising. It sounded like a moaning woman. In the dark, clouds began to build and obscure the fire doves along the horizon.

The ship's electrical system was shut off. Below decks candles were lit and held by hand.

Above the *Trident* the sky whipped itself into a glittering frosty green foam. Snow fell in hand-sized flakes onto the ship and the sea. The air chilled, then became as warm as a mid-summer night thick with moisture. Water dribbled down the bulkheads.

Ahead, kilometers off, a mound of sea was rising. It stretched across the entire horizon.

"That's it," Prekari said.

The bow jumped and the ship screamed. Rivets popped along the deck like bullets. With the speed of a cargo boom hauling a light load, the wave brought the ship to its mammoth peak, bucked it about in white water and foam, and twisted it around. It lurched sideways into the trough like a toboggan down a slope of snow, veering and weaving, water pouring over its decks. The mizzenmast snapped free from the poop deck and toppled over, breaking lines and driving the spanker spar through the steel plates of the deck like an arrow. Barthel stared at the splintered shaft. It was barely a meter from where he was strapped down.

The dog-tail waves that followed bounced the *Trident* vigorously, but she took them with little trouble. In the wake of the big wave the water was churning and boiling, and things were rising from the sea bottom which had lain undisturbed for centuries. A barnacled and crumpled wreck bobbled to the surface almost under the *Trident*, masts and hull above water for several seconds before it sank like a stone. The sea was silty, and big gouts of bubbling mud exploded. Tangled knots of seaweed floated like the hair of drowned women.

Aching and shaken, the crew untied themselves and scrambled on deck to see what there was to do. They shook their heads in disbelief. Some cried—men, women, and children alike. People were hugging each other like long lost friends.

"It's not over yet," Bar-Woten said. No one listened—they were wild with elation and danced on the deck as the air grew moist again. Snow fell again, drifting peacefully to the deck. A snapping cold wind raced over the ship and painted hoarfrost on the rigging.

The captain called from the bridge for all to brace. A second wave was coming, larger than the first.

They had only a few minutes to get below and tie themselves in again. The *Trident* took water in her bilges faster than the pumps could remove it and rode lower by a meter, listing slightly as she turned into the approaching mountain.

Kiril helped tie the last errant child and took hold of the edges of a beam, knowing he had no time to rope himself. His stomach seemed to fall to his feet. Outside was a sound none had ever heard before—the insane deafening roar of atoms being destroyed. A flash covered the sky.

The ship plunged. The bulkhead of an aft compartment separated and bent like the metal in a child's toy. Kiril swung around and lost his grip, bounced off a secured collection of crates, and fell somewhere, he didn't know where. It was dark at the bottom.

13

Golumbine was almost unrecognizable. The wharves and bunds were gone or covered with mud and silt. The long boathouses were shards of wet and splintered wood, and the boats were scattered wreckage. The island was quiet as a tomb. No one moved. The ship drifted into the filthy harbor, fragments of wood and corpses of animals and humans bumping against her bow. The city of Mappu was not visible from the ocean and may have been protected by its surround of hills, but they could see no activity at all. To a height of fifty meters the wooded hills were ragged and stripped.

Dat and one of her guardians were still upright smeared with weed and mud to the waist. The other serpent column wasn't visible. The daylight was milky and incomplete; the north was gray and dark.

Deathly tired, retching from the smell of corruption in the warm still air, the people of the *Trident* watched as their ship dropped anchor.

Bar-Woten came on deck. His face was pale and lined with grease and dirt. Barthel stood by the railing on the main deck and stared listlessly at the island.

"He has some broken ribs," the Ibisian said. Barthel

nodded. "Something may be wrong with his head too. The doctor doesn't know for sure."

There was no tide to scour the beaches or take the flotsam out to sea. Only a mild seaward current flowed through the harbor. In a few more days the whole area would be an aquatic pesthole rife with disease, unless something was done to clear it out.

In the early afternoon, Bar-Woten went with the first boat to go ashore. They scrambled up a sagging wooden dock that had been driven half its length ashore and stood on the crumbling remains of the log and brick bund. A few birds scolded them from the naked trees as they walked on the ragged roadway inland.

The waves had burrowed up the inland passage with concentrated force, leaving the hills spattered with mud and twisted foliage. But the water had spent its force against the great stone boulder that formed a partial gateway to the valley of Mappu. It had coursed down the highway and spilled into the river that ran through the city. Mappu itself looked a little shaken, and some of its buildings were cracked and leaning precariously, but on the whole it had survived well. Only a few islanders were in the city, however. They were old or very young and looked dazed, with wild, staring eyes. They could only point and say everyone had gone to Dat.

The shore party halted at the palace gates and reconnoitered. Bar-Woten and three others were instructed by the first mate to take the dirt path to the eastern peninsula about ten kilometers away and see how many islanders were actually at the statues. The others would go deeper into the valley and determine how many had hidden in the inland caves beyond Mappu.

Dark clouds were building to the south and rushing with unusal haste toward the island. Bar-Woten watched thunderheads grow, visibly billowing and darkening. Sheets of silent lightning played between them.

The party was between two walls of thick, buggy jungle when the first downpour hit. Taking shelter beneath a broad, leafy ironwood tree, they waited as marble-sized drops of water pummeled the forest and roadway. The storm abated to a fine drizzle, fading the trees into rustling gray giants and decorating the leaves with crystal beads. The bird noises resumed. Insects rose in puffs and blasts, haunting every step in the ankle-deep mud. Large spiders, red and tan, crossed the path with high-prancing steps and challenged the hikers courageously. The Ibisian forged ahead and shooed them aside with a broken palm frond. In a few minutes the end of the frond was sticky with webbing.

Two of the party were women, one middle-aged and graying with knotted muscles on her arms and calves, tough as any man; the other slender and young with a close-cut shag of hair. The second man was an engine-watch officer, ten years younger than Bar-Woten, but just as knowledgeable in the ways of jungles. They swapped short, breathless stories on jungle life. Bar-Woten told of the years he'd spent in the Pais Vermagne, searching for the city of the First-born. It was the first any had heard of his long trek, and they asked lots of questions, some of them pointed. He deftly avoided incriminating answers.

The path emerged on a white sand beach that had avoided the major impact of the deluge. They walked across the hard-packed, damp sand for a half hour, then crossed a muddy jungle stream from the hills. The path picked up again a few steps beyond and led them over a rise into the valley where the statues stood.

Dat had been imposing from the sea; now she was overwhelming. The waves had toppled one of her guardians. The serpent column lay at her feet, half-buried in mud and foliage. Seated in silence around the valley, on the fallen column, at the base of Dat, and even on the crest of the cliffs twenty or thirty meters higher, were at least ten thousand people. They stared with wide, clear eyes at the goddess's face, hands folded in their laps. The tiny King and Queen sat among them, incense bearers nearby.

Bar-Woten understood. He sat on an unoccupied rock and motioned for the others to follow his example. Together they stared at Dat and thought their own thoughts.

They were all lucky to be alive.

Kiril's chest was tightly wrapped with bandages, and it hurt him to breathe. There was a funny dislocated feeling around his shoulders. He couldn't focus both eyes on a single object for very long. Vague shapes moved around him in the dark.

I'm in the infirmary, he told himself. Something happened to me. I might have fallen down stairs. Slipped.

He remembered nothing about the waves.

He dreamed fuzzy dreams for a long time—months it seemed—about riding the balloons in Mediweva, reading the Obelisk texts, meeting and becoming friendly with and loving Elena, spending afternoons in the park around the promenade in the village of Gidalha, where the birds sang even past dark and the air smelled of frangipani from the village censers breathing out their holiday smells.

He talked to the doctor and his nurse occasionally, but there were a lot of small injuries to be treated, and cases much more serious than his own. Bar-Woten and Barthel were both on the island, so he spent most of his time alone.

The sounds of riveting and hammering and sawing came to him day and night. He slowly remembered what had happened.

He overheard that one third of Golumbine's population, seventeen thousand people, had died in the waves. Most of the native boats had been swamped at sea or wrecked ashore. Twenty crewmen on the *Trident* had been badly hurt and three were dead.

He slept. He led a disjointed existence for two weeks.

The day finally came when he was allowed to walk by himself and go on deck. He looked north. It was still gray, but the south was bright and warm and inviting. The island was disheveled, with an intent, serious look of recovery. People were repairing the docks and bund. Long lines of them carried pails of bricks and mortar back and forth in an endless stream. Masons applied and cemented, working by torchlight at night.

The smell of death was almost gone. Boats still cruised the harbor, dredging for bodies and taking them out to sea for deep-water burial. The majority of the flotsam had been salvaged for rebuilding boats.

Only a few floating tree trunks provided a hazard to navigation. The water was a clear blue-green again.

The weather had changed. Winds from the north were colder, and everyone on the *Trident* knew that meant only one thing. The Obelisk that had once risen high over Weggismarche and Pallasta and the other countries below the Pale Seas was now gone. What that had done to the *Trident*'s homeland none could say—but they weren't optimistic.

The very thought that an Obelisk could fall was shaking. Added to the starry sky of nine months past, it meant nothing was going to be as it had been. But how meany more disasters would hit them?

Kiril had known things were awry for two and a half years, ever since Elena had been changed. It was a matter of escalation, not beginnings.

The *Trident* needed repairs which would take at least two months. In that time those who weren't directly involved with the work were given leave to help on the island. Shoreline communities had to be rebuilt from the ground up, and in some cases repopulated.

In the wake of the disaster the island no longer mourned. Rather a mood of frenetic work prevailed. By some fluke there were more men on the island than women now, by about two to one. This didn't conflict with the past at all, as polyandry had been an accepted practice. But it created a host of problems for the men.

Kiril spent his last days of recovery touring the island, walking or riding on the half-repaired roads, and visiting the sites where the *Trident*'s crew was helping rebuild.

He stayed for two days in Mappu as a consultant in reshelving the religious library. The second day he sat

in the tumble of stone shelves and scrolls with a group
of priest-initiates and explained the practice of setting
up a card catalog, stumbling between Teutan and ru-
dimentary Golumbine.

A black-haired, umber-skinned woman entered the
library and snapped her fingers commandingly. They
all looked up, Kiril frowning. She wore a sari-like dress
that covered her from ankle to shoulder. Her expression was mild and gentle, and when she spoke she
used the proper words of apology, but she obviously
expected their complete attention.

A formal choosing of husbands would begin at dusk
in Mappu's ritual plaza. All unchosen males were required to be there. She added, with a neutral glance
at Kiril, that foreigners were also invited. "The obliga-
tions, in any case, will be temporary," she explained to
him in Teutan. Then she smiled, turned delicately,
and walked out.

It was the last thing Kiril wanted to be involved in.
The initiates buzzed with interest and speculation. It
took him some minutes to bring the discussion back to
the catalog.

Bar-Woten and Barthel walked across the half-
finished bund and hired a taxi to take them to the
ritual plaza. They were passing through a side street
in Mappu, their driver hissing his animal on and flapping the reins, when they saw Kiril. They ordered the
taxi to stop and invited him to join them. He was too
tired to think much about where they were going. He
assumed they were on their way to supper. He
climbed into the carriage, and the taxi picked up
speed.

The ritual plaza was a broad, open square paved in

ochre stone bricks, with a deep communal cistern at
its center and a rise of stone seats at one end. Thousands of years ago the plaza had been the scene of
sacrifices, whether animal or human the Golumbines
were reluctant to say. Now it served as a civic center
when the island council met.

The seats were filled with bustling and chattering
women, dressed in ceremonious red and gold wrappings, their hair flowing over their shoulders and their
eyes bright with interest. The plaza was empty, but
crowds of men clustered at both sides looking anxious
and nervous. The taxi let the three out at the edge of
the plaza, Kiril realized they weren't going to dinner.

"What are we doing here?" he asked quietly. Bar-
Woten grinned and said nothing. Too tired to put up
any fuss, he stood with them, willing to watch the
proceedings but not to participate. His ribs still ached
a little.

The late afternoon was still warm and sultry. Birds
squawked in the jungle beyond the plaza's boundary.
A tall priest dressed in green walked to the top of the
wall around the well and called for order in a loud,
clear voice. When he had everybody's attention he
told the crowd on all three sides that the choosing
could begin.

Kiril wearily tried to find a hint of moral fault with
what was going on, but couldn't. He'd seen too much
grief and misery in the streets of Mappu in the last
few weeks to grudge this organic respite. There was
anxiety in the crowd, but also joy and anticipation. He
couldn't visualize what the result would be—a series
of ritual marriages? Or arranged orgies to stimulate a
new, fresh tide of children? It all seemed very remote.
He watched with objective interest.

The men at the opposite side of the plaza stepped forward and arranged themselves in front of the stone seats, each standing two steps from his neighbor to be seen clearly. The first row of women went among the men and looked them over sharply, haggling with each other. For a spectator it wasn't entrancing. All together around six thousand people filled the plaza, with twice as many men as there were women.

The haggling continued until dusk. Torches were set in stands along the plaza to light the proceedings. The women made their choices from the first group. About three hundred men went away unchosen.

Golumbine priests then urged the second group to take its position. Kiril was caught up in the crowd, something he hadn't bargained for. He was pushed forward despite his protests. "I'm not supposed to be here," he said, but the men surrounding him thought he was only trying to find a better frontline position. They laughed and held him to his ground. Barthel and Bar-Woten were lost in the press, and he couldn't see them.

He shrugged his coat back onto his shoulders. It was useless. No one would choose him anyway. The men fell quiet as the women started to pass among them. Most of the women smiled at Kiril, but paid little attention—he was from the *Trident*, not a native. It wasn't wise to get involved with a sailor.

He felt depressed after an hour under the dark sky. Few fire doves were visible. Brighter ones would blink into view in a few minutes, and others would rise, but for the moment it was dark with only torchlight to guide the women.

One girl a few years younger than Kiril stopped and tried to talk to him. It was no good. He knew very little dialect, and she knew nothing in Teutan beyond amenities. She looked him over frostily and moved on.

Irritated and nervous he shifted on his feet and wondered when it would be over. His legs were aching and his chest was scratchy beneath his bandages.

He ignored the next woman who looked at him. He held out his arm when she asked, then blinked and looked at her more closely. She spoke excellent Teutan. She was the woman who'd made the announcement in the library. Her teeth flashed at him, and she asked how he was feeling.

"Fine," he said, his mouth going dry. She looked him over thoroughly like a doctor, but with less coarseness than the other women. Finally she took his hand and put it on her waist, the signal she had chosen him.

"But I'm not in the—the competition," he said.

"Come with me."

He passed Bar-Woten, who raised an eyebrow, then grinned broadly and grunted deep in his throat.

"Damn you!" Kiril whispered. "Get me out of this!"

"I am Ual," the woman said. "I like you because I think you're probably pretty smart. You smart?"

"Dumb as an ox," Kiril said.

"I don't *think* so!" she said, her voice rising to a pretty peak.

"I'll have to go back on the ship, so this is all useless."

She shook her head, no, and he suddenly found himself willing. Something simply snapped and he caught the spirit, and his body grew warm and he liked the touch of her hand.

"You'll be excused for a while," she said. "You work here now anyway."

They left the plaza and followed a twisting, dark road through Mappu. Hundreds of fire doves were out like glowing insects now. He wanted to take her then and there, with an insane pressure he could hardly control. But she kept his hand loosely in hers and led him through a gate into a courtyard.

"I don't feel too well," something made him say. She smiled back, and he knew he was lying.

14

The inside of the courtyard was paved with tile and had a fountain in the middle, a bronze dish supported by stone lions so old they were almost shapeless. Lamplight came through the upper windows of the house at the end of the yard. A jagged crack ran from the rounded top of the door frame to a window above. It all looked as old as the fountain. Next to it, Ual was as fresh and young as a flower.

They went through the door and stood in a hallway, which crossed the front of the house. There were doors at either end. He asked why the hall had no door in the middle, and she said that was to keep the *gingerii* out—demons. Demons could only travel in a straight line. She quickly demonstrated that there was no way a demon could get from the door to the end of the hall in a straight line in either direction. Kiril nodded. She led him to the right and opened the door with an iron key tied around her wrist.

She left him standing alone in a small, bare room with a window at eye level in the outer wall. He sat on a smooth wooden bench, crossing his legs. Elena came to mind, and he frowned. Something feral was working in him. He turned his guilt into a kind of anger at Elena; she had no right to expect him to be inhumanly chaste.

"This is the household of my brother, Hualao," she told him when she returned. "He died in the waves." Kiril apologized, and she looked at him curiously.

"You had nothing to do with it."

"But I'm sorry he's dead."

"If he wasn't dead, you wouldn't be here. Your ship would have sailed away, and I'd have never even thought about choosing you."

Kiril nodded, though he didn't understand. He followed her into a high-ceilinged room filled with a stone hearth, a heavy plush rug, and comfortably padded rattan furniture.

"I'm a virgin," she said. He nodded agreeably until he realized what she'd said. He felt stupid and clumsy. This was a sensuous ocean island—weren't all girls soon experienced here? His nervousness trebled.

"But you won't be able—" he started and found he had nothing to follow.

"Hm?"

"I'm sorry," he said.

"You're very sorry all the time."

"I'll be sleeping out here," he said. In Mediweva husbands always spent the first few nights sleeping separately from their wives. It supposedly built up friendship and confidence and confirmed the relationship in the eyes of God.

"You'll be cold. You don't want to sleep out here."

"Why did you choose me? I can't stay in Golumbine. I'd make a very poor husband."

"You don't like me?" she asked. "I'm very likable. Lots of men want me."

"I like you—I want you very much."

"You don't sound sure."

"How old are you, Ual?"

"Marriage age."

"I mean, how many years?"

"That is one word I've never been able to understand."

They took seats next to each other on a divan with cotton cushions. Kiril told her what a year was, and she laughed. Without Obelisk texts to influence a person, Hegira was virtually timeless, divided only into night and day. Seasons weren't important when the prevailing winds were warm and the currents brought a tropical surge day in, day out.

"I am many, many days old," she said. "I must be many years old, maybe fifty."

"No," he said. "You can't be fifty. I'd say you're about twenty. Maybe twenty-two."

"That must be your age."

"About" he said. "I'm twenty-one, very young."

"Marriage age."

"But I can't stay."

"That's okay. I will have many other husbands, perhaps before you leave."

He held his hands together between his knees and swallowed. He'd almost forgotten. Something ached inside him, and it wasn't his healing rib cage.

"I'm not used to that, Ual," he said. "Where I come from, a man can only have one wife."

"Same here, sometimes," she said.

"But a woman can only have one husband."

"Oh." She looked at his hands and put her hand on them. "Listen. I'm an important woman here. Lots of men want to marry me. But I'm important enough I won't need to have more husbands if you don't want them, until after you go. Ship will stay here another . . ." she paused. "Thirty or forty days. Part of a year. I can wait. I like you enough to wait."

He didn't know what to do. But someone inside of him did. He held her hand up to his and kissed it. It reminded him of kissing Elena's hand, but not in an unpleasant way. It was like all women were wonderfully the same, with the same ability to soothe and attract . . . and hurt terribly if he didn't handle things right. If he did something wrong. He felt very mixed up, but wonderful. "I'm honored," he whispered.

"That's the way," she said. "Now I know why I picked you. You're a virgin too!"

Kiril opened and closed his mouth like a fish. He resented her implication all the more because it was true. He looked at her steadfastly. "Why would you want to choose a virgin? Both of us will be stumbling in the dark."

"There will be no advantages. . . . Both will learn."

She had moved no closer to him, but the heat of her body and her subtle perfume were already bothering him. There were many texts on the Obelisks that gave intimate details of the love habits of the First-born. There was no reason to think things were any different on the far island of Golumbine. But did they kiss with their lips?

It was necessary for him to find out.

They did, and apparently by long tradition.

He was still nervous as she stroked the back of his neck and nibbled at his nose. But he noted with some pride that it wasn't a debilitating anxiety. He knew little about disrobing a young woman, but Golumbine's fashions weren't nearly as difficult to remove as Mediweva's had been. He ruefully remembered hav-

ing tried several times with Elena. If the stays and
girdles had been less restraining she might have given
in. But he had been ham-handed, unaware of the puz-
zles that gave easy access when solved. Both had re-
treated in discouragement.

Ual did not retreat. She helped. He grew accus-
tomed to her willingness, but it took some time to get
used to her unnerving familiarity with his own clothing and his own person.

He thought of Elena, not with guilt, but with a
sharp, grieving pain. By rights this should have been
her night, her privilege—their privilege—and not the
smiling, willing joy of an umber-skinned woman in a
land Elena had never heard of. Knowing this, and
feeling the stab, he understood with more than his
mind that he had no choice.

All of Golumbine was demanding a rebirth. Who
was he to resist? He went with her to a room lit by
small oil lamps, where there was a thick, soft mat
woven of rattan and cotton yarn covered with a sheet
of fine linen. The sheet was printed with blocks and
circles of purple and brown. As she removed her final
garment, a small pair of pants with a skirt around
them, and turned to face him, he felt his entire chest
alternately weakening and growing strong with the
push-pull of his heart and lungs. It was a flutter he'd
never felt before, a thick-running excitement that was
a mixture of terror and pride.

He was afraid of hurting her. She pulled him down,
and her eyes were so dark in the dim lamplight that
he couldn't see their whites, just narrow gaps of
brown, almost black. Her mouth was open with all
her teeth showing.

Later, her hips and thighs crimsoned, she took his

hand and moved him off the bed. She gathered up the cloth and cut it into small strips with a sharp knife. Then in the sitting room she soaked it in oil and put it in the fire. She squatted before it, an awesome, youthful idol, flames mirrored in her eyes.

She cleaned both of them off with a soft wet rag and spread another sheet like the first. Kiril found it hard to go to sleep quickly. He stayed awake an hour or more longer than Ual, staring into the dark.

15

Birds rose from the lake, pink and white and midnight blue, as Bar-Woten plunged his paddle into the water and scooted the reed boat along. Jungle circled the lake and even extended into it, with long grotesqueries of twisted roots. Birds and aquatic lizards flocked across the roots in squawking conflict. The sky was a hot, pale blue. The north was no longer dark. Through a smoked glass a bright band of light could be seen extending from the western Obelisk and widening to form an ovoid where the northern Obelisk had been.

A head with glittering, opalescent eyes rose in the water where he was about to dip his paddle, making him jerk his arm back. The head vanished, and water sprayed with the swish of a tail. This was no lake for unaided swimmers. Insects long as a finger scurried over it and dipped below to pierce small fish and tadpoles with wicked mandibles. They could just as easily bite through an unwary hand. White snakes—a delicate side dish for the Golumbines—gathered in floating lacework colonies to swim and bask.

The lake was a soup of life. It was tepid and brackish at one end, clogged with leech-infested reeds and matted algae. But it did not smell too offensive because the wind was fresh and strong. The wind dried off the sweat of his paddling and made the jungle hum and whistle. Drifts of spider web floated from the trees.

He brought the boat up onto a dirt embankment and pulled it out of the water. Then he sat on a mossy rock to think. His foot found a hold in the spotted gray stone, and he bent to examine the niche. It was more than a rock—it was a head. Worn gray eyes peered at him, eyebrows cracked and covered with lichen. The stone nose was half-buried in thick damp soil. Ageless idols were not rare here, but it still fascinated him. He had often dreamed of exploring long-deserted cities. Perhaps temples existed in the jungle that could begin to slake that thirst. But the deep jungle wasn't recommended for inexpert visitors.

He had borrowed the boat and crossed the lake to find a place to sit and think alone and in relative silence. But now that he was alone he couldn't concentrate. His mind kept drifting off like the spider webs. Some carried him into the past, and he didn't want to follow them at all. That way led to blood and cruelty and mind-blanked hatred. It also reminded him of a great love for Sulay.

He still felt sad for Sulay. The memories welled up, and he couldn't put them aside: The day he had fought with the bear and lost his eye, and that evening as the pharmacists had bandaged him . . . Sulay had stood over him in the dark and firelight with the dark forest all around, chuckling and reassuring. "You're Bear-killer now . . . Woten would be proud, and so would the Thunder-Bearer, Eloshim."

Years later, as an aide to the general, he had been given the pick of the captured Khemites to choose a servant from. Tired from the fighting and feeling dirty with blood and self-anger, Bar-Woten had recognized a face among the children. Barthel—"Servant of Bar," originally named Amma bin Akka—had been small, dark, and scrappy with more spirit and fear and hate than Bar-Woten had ever thought he could control. But the young Khemite had taken to Bar-Woten as if to a second father, imitating him and absorbing all he had to teach, although retaining his Momadan faith. For years Bar-Woten had trusted the Khemite not to plunge a knife into his back. There was good reason for him to try, Bar-Woten knew—but the Khemite didn't know the reason.

And Bar-Woten would never tell, because his stomach heaved at the memory. It was just as well that Barthel had hidden under reed baskets that day in Khem and seen so little.

An insect crawled up his leg, and he let it climb onto his finger, chancing that it might sting or prick, but it did nothing, and he set it off on the jungle floor.

He brought out his leather pouch and ate. What was most terrible of all was that he didn't feel nearly as guilty as he should. He took his pain with a sort of zest. He knew he could repeat the past at any time, because though forbidding, it wasn't nearly as frightening as what lay ahead. Establishing familiar territory in the future was necessary, even though the landmarks should be blood and destruction.

Bar-Woten shook his head slowly, chewing on his piece of fruit. He packed his waste into the leather pouch and put the boat in the river to continue his journey.

Golumbine offered any number of marvels to the casual eye. There were deep green gorges slashed with long plumes of waterfalls where circular rainbows dazzled. There were multicolored reptile herds, some carnivorous, but most not, which stalked through the forest on their hind feet, hunting or browsing on the lower branches and ferns. Butterflies wide as two hands thumb-to-thumb bobbed in and out of shadow. There were marble quarries and quartz hillsides.

And there was Mappu itself, where men were in abundance, and neither he nor Barthel found themselves in much demand. He smiled at that, thinking of Kiril's distress. They hadn't met since.

He was envious. He'd grown a little bored with the women of the *Trident*.

Barthel looked at the maps laid out before him on a forecastle capstan and drew his finger along the Bicht of Weggismarche. There was a small circle that showed the former position of the Obelisk. He used a pencil to sketch in the probable path of the fall.

Their trade route took them several broad curves from Columbine to southern Weggismarche. Depending on what they found after delivering their chief cargo—saffron and several other ton-lots of spice—they'd make a brief journey into the Pale Seas to pick up goods in the port of Dambapur, the farthest northern city of Weggismarche's tiny sister-state, Nin. Then they'd sail with the currents to the southeast and begin another long circle, which, in five or six years, would again end in Weggismarche.

If there was nothing left of Weggismarche their plans would have to change, of course. At any rate Barthel knew that Bar-Woten, Kiril, and himself would probably leave the ship before then. They might travel along the coast of the Pale Seas, though the map was unspecific about what lay in those regions beyond a cursory trace of probable coastal zones.

He was reluctant to leave the *Trident*. He'd learned a lot on the ship and gained some independence from the Bey by being able to do his own work and think his own thoughts. But he knew his loyalty was still too strong to break. He'd go where the Bey went, and Kiril probably would too.

He'd seen Kiril with his "wife" the day before at one of Mappu's vegetable markets. He'd looked contented. That puzzled Barthel. Changes in men's moods or mores always puzzled him. The Bey had been the way he was since Barthel had known him, given allowances for times and strenuous circumstances. But Kiril, closer to Barthel's age, seemed much more changeable. Barthel wondered if he himself could show fluctuations as broad. He didn't think so.

Work on the port hull of the *Trident* was nearly finished. In a few weeks the ship would be ready to leave, and they'd all have to detach themselves from Golumbine. He was glad he didn't have many detachments to make.

Captain Prekari was making his usual midafternoon inspection of the repairs, carrying rolls of ship's plans in metal tubes, when Bar-Woten came aboard. He went to his cabin and saluted the captain in passing, dropped his goods on the narrow double bunk that he shared with Barthel—who took the upper berth—and went aft to shower under freshwater pumps. He didn't trust the baywater yet. No one did. The saltwater pumps were detached for the time they'd spend in the harbor.

He soaked himself down and used lye soap to scrub off.

Kiril came aboard two hours later looking tired and irritable. Barthel talked with him and showed him the map course, but didn't ask any questions. The evening meal was quiet. Those who had worked all day on the ship were tired, and those who had been ashore all day looked equally fatigued.

Just after dusk Kiril lay on a lower berth in the cabin he shared with three other men and listened to someone striking up a dance with pipes and tambourine on the quarterdeck. He was too tired to think much, though Ual came to mind before he went to sleep. He'd been helping two of her half-brothers repair the cracks in the house that day. It had taken a great deal of mortar mixing and masonry, and his hands were raw. He'd told her he had to be on board this evening for watch, too weary to face the planned family festivities after the day was done. Still, just before sleep, he missed her warmth and wished he'd stayed behind.

He dreamed about walking with Elena to the temple of Dat in the older section of Mappu. She offered up torn strips of cloth, and the statue bent to accept them with a flaming hand. The statue was not dark-bronze, but mirror-bright silver; and the cloth strips turned to ice and melted away in the flames, hissing. He woke in the morning with a drained feeling and wondered what Elena would have been doing, in any case, on Golumbine.

The morale of the ship was at a low ebb. They had no idea what had happened in Weggismarche, whether there was any country to return to or not. They feared not.

Some fighting broke out, and the animosities they caused were difficult to settle. The captain began to avoid direct contact with the crew, which Bar-Woten knew was a standard tactic in times of unresolvable tension. Work on the ship slowed somewhat, and the quality of the work declined.

More and more of the crew were withdrawn from helping the Golumbines and assigned to repair details on the *Trident*, allowing shorter shifts. Kiril sweated for a day the possibility he would be withdrawn also, but he remained.

At midday, his library instruction duties over, he went to Ual's clan home and helped fix the family meal. It was everybody's duty to contribute something to the late afternoon repast. Kiril was no good as a cook, so he helped with the cleaning and basic preparation of the raw food. Ual and one sister did most of the cooking.

The family was huge by any standard. The relations of the various members to each other were difficult to understand and impossible for Kiril to remember. He stumbled along as best he could and tried to keep his astonishment and indignation in check. Family standards for breeding were much looser than in Mediweva. Dat, he learned from Ual, was the product of her own extratemporal union with the ocean god, Nepheru-Shaka. She was her own mother then, and her own daughter. Nepheru-Shaka was conceived (again out of time) by Dat and the island god, Ashlok—both of whom were female, but Ashlok less definitely so. From this Trinity—with Ashlok as the only unbegotten and unexplained part—came all the other forces, *gingerii*, minor gods, and the seventy-nine Notions that comprised the loose pantheon of Golumbine. It was a very intellectual religion, quite static. By any definition of culture the Golumbine population should have crumbled into formless bands and gone through the agonies of cultural renaissance long ago. But the culture was stable and showed no signs of decay. Kiril, struggling to ignore the lessons of Firstborn history as recorded on the Obelisks, speculated the Golumbines were flexible in other ways. Certainly the family group was flexible. They seemed to follow the example of their gods—first cousins were allowed to marry; even, in certain circumstances, brother and sister.

The generic name of Ual's family was Punapilhi, with the ending "hi" inexpressibly whistled. Within that group name, seldom used, were other names denoting people living together under one roof, people wishing to be named as a subgroup for various reasons, associations of artisans within the family, and other relations that escaped Kiril.

Ual herself was directly involved with family planning. She was a representative in what the *Trident*'s crew called "the Rebirth Committee." Its main function was to keep Golumbine's diverse family groups together and encourage the production of healthy children. They had a crude but surprisingly effective method of family counseling on good breeding. To an extent this made them matchmakers.

Ual's natural father accepted Kiril without comment. Ual had several family fathers—her natural father was not even her favorite. All her fathers—and at one count Kiril found six—had been husbands to her mother, who was a pleasant, plump old woman, no great beauty now, but handsome and jovial. Kiril took a shine to her.

Ual treated Kiril in public like a favorite brother, and in private little differently, but with extended liberties. His state of husbandship was not stressed, nor formalized by ritual, for he wasn't yet a father. She didn't discourage him from setting up relationships with other females in the family group, but Kiril had no inclination to do so. The whole arrangement was at times a strain on him. After a month of "marriage," he slept aboard the *Trident* more often. He disliked himself for not fitting in, but he knew the reasons why. His whole being was alien to their way of life.

It was difficult to face the fact—a very un-Kristian fact—that there were many ways of being happy, prosperous, and pious in human experience. Some of those ways contradicted one another.

As his disenchantment increased, his love for Ual also increased. Halfhearted, sick with conflict, he struggled with himself. He couldn't let things ride until the *Trident* offered her own solution. He had to act sooner.

Ual did not become pregnant in the first month. Her period came, something Kiril knew very little about, and she was sequestered until the menstrual flow had ceased. This had never been the custom in Mediweva, but Kiril accepted it. It gave him time to think clearly.

When she came out of seclusion, her work with the Rebirth Committee absorbed her for a few more days. They saw very little of each other. Then Kiril managed to pull her away from her omnipresent family, from her position on the Committee, but not from her preoccupation with thoughts of both. At first she only half listened as he tried to explain his difficulties.

They sat in the empty vegetable market of Mappu

in the late afternoon of a religious holiday. A faint breeze scattered bits of dried twigs and leaves across the ground, sounding like the tick of dogs' claws on pavement. He told her he was finding it hard to be happy.

"You've said nothing before," she told him.

"I've been trying to explain it to myself. I can't."

"Because you're going, that's why you're unhappy."

"That may be. But also because I can't fit into what you do, with your family and all. I'm a wanderer, but I have a lot of solid things in my life that keep me from being like you."

"Oh," she said. "But you leave soon anyway. Enjoy while you can."

He shook his head. It was impossible to explain.

"I would like one thing," Ual said quietly, looking up at him to watch his reaction. "I would like to take advantage of an offer that will be helpful when you leave. A man has offered to be a husband to me, and the alliance of our families would be desirable."

"After I'm gone you won't have to ask for permission."

"I would marry him before, but I made a promise to you. You would have to release me from that."

Kiril stared at her.

"He will not be a mating husband until after you've gone," she assured him.

He was scandalized. "I can't allow that," he said, knowing he was being despicable. "That's not right."

"But we love each other now."

"You love ME!"

"Yes."

"Then why don't you try to stop me from going?"

"I like you. I won't stop you on your path."

"But if you loved me you'd try to keep me for as long as you could, against everything."

"I love the pictures in the sky at night when the fire doves draw," she said. "But I can't stop them from changing, and each night they are different."

"There has to be something, something *wrong* when two people don't wish to have each other for as long as they can."

"I do want you."

"Not forever."

"I'm not sure of that word. I've studied it. I don't think there is a forever."

"As long as we live."

"Ah! But after we die Dat makes sure we never meet again in other bodies to mate. It is a rule of nature that all things must leave each other. I cannot fight that. You cannot. Nepheru-Shaka will take you away to Weggismarche, and you will have things to do there."

Kiril had nothing to say. His brain was a knot of thoughts, all of them valid, all ridiculous.

"And you have told me," Ual continued, "that you have to rescue a person you love very deeply. I cannot stop you from that."

"Ual, that has nothing to do with—" He stopped himself.

It did. It had everything to do with what he was doing now. He didn't care about Elena now. He wanted only Ual, and he wanted her away from her family, away from Bar-Woten and Barthel, from the *Trident*, even from Golumbine, away in some nowhere without conflict. That was the only way he could have her, keep her, the way he wanted her. Kiril knew that was hopelessly immature and destructive. It hurt that he couldn't stop himself from wanting it.

They would destroy each other even in ideal circumstances. She was like a fish out of water when isolated from her family. Taken away from the journey to find Elena's double, he would be a stripling youth again, without strength or purpose. He would wander from life to life and probably not find happiness even in the best of times with Ual.

He held his hands out in front of him in a shrug and told her it couldn't go on. "I don't feel right about it," he said. She became exasperated.

"You don't know what love is!" she said. "You want everything to last forever."

He nodded.

"So you would stop us from loving now, from helping to rebuild, because you will leave. I don't understand that."

There was nothing for him to do but get angry. "You'll have a dozen husbands after me," he said, his voice grinding low in his throat. "Why don't you just forget me, write me off as a bad job?"

"You are senseless now," she said.

"No doubt. It hurts me to do this."

"It hurts me to watch you."

They sat in the shade of a wide, tall fern in the vegetable market and looked at each other for a few seconds. Kiril felt removed from time. The myriad pressures all added up to one push, which he was following as surely as an arrow flies from its string.

She stood up and started to walk away.

"No," Kiril said, reaching out to hold her hand. "I don't want you to go without understanding. I want to help both of us understand. You're the first woman I've ever had. I'm glad for that. You did nothing to hurt me. But after a while I'd be like a rock around your neck. You'd want to take other husbands, and I wouldn't let you. Even anticipating that makes me mad at myself, and with you. Because you can't be what I want you to be."

"Can anyone?" she asked, a quick coldness in her voice.

He spoke softly and his words were sure. "Not now. But you especially can't be. I think we have to leave each other. Let's not do it with bitterness."

"There is no other way," she said. "Otherwise we will not leave for good. A good hunter always makes a clean kill."

"Neither of us are hunting."

"You! You are hunting."

It had to end in anger or it would start up again; it had to be killed. He knew that was what Ual meant. She was turning her disappointment into indignation. Blaming him was the only way.

His shoulders dropped slightly. "I'm sorry," he said.

"You, you are always sorry."

Then she was gone, and the weight was gone, and something like clarity returned to his thoughts. But his shoulders wouldn't rise again, and he couldn't stand straight. He'd found the final solution, and he hated it.

He returned to the *Trident*. The broken mast was being replaced and new rigging was being strung. Darkness came quickly, and candles and torches were lit on the bund like processions of fire doves.

16

The *Trident* steamed out of the harbor with bright sky and calm water to greet her. She was stained with rust along her hull, and some of her sails were patchwork, but her engines were running smoothly and her methane tanks were full. To Bar-Woten she didn't sound the same—her squeaks and groans and snaps came from different areas with different rhythm—but she took the wind well when it came up, and nothing ominous sounded. She was seaworthy again.

Golumbine drifted to the south. By evening they couldn't see the island any more. They were sailing into the dark blue seas that marked the northern waters of the Bicht av Genevar. Out of the warm currents surrounding Golumbine, the air grew chill. High clouds of ice crystals glowed overhead as the last of daylight faded; herringbone, mare's tail, lacework, and fly's wing. To Kiril it looked sometimes as though cryptic messages were being written in the sky, almost decipherable.

Barthel and Avra and two navigation officers studied the morning glare of the light above the fallen Obelisk, trying to determine how it grew bright and why it faded. Barthel had the uncomfortable feeling it was no natural thing they were watching—not the work of

Allah, but something a shade less exalted, though no less impressive.

Bar-Woten worked for several days finding small leaks in the methane tanks where they'd been stressed. He worked silently, putting his whole body into it, glad to be traveling again. When his duty was over he went to the prow and stood with one foot resting on the bowsprit clamps, staring north with eyes squinted as though riddling what lay ahead. Sometimes he shivered and went to his cabin before darkness set in. None of what he saw in the hazy distance pleased him.

And nothing of what they found in the Bicht was encouraging. Most of the small islands were now barren deserts of sand and mud with patches of salt grass. The larger ones had been ravaged not only by waves and quakes, but by what looked like war. Entire villages had been haphazardly rebuilt, only to be put to the torch. No trading was possible where the only inhabitants on the islands were half-dead old women and belly-bloated children. The *Trident* gave aid where she could, but more often than not she had to leave at full speed with desperate rag-tag ships in pursuit.

The farther north they sailed, the more discouraged they became. The voyage had gone sour. The captain stayed isolated, and all orders were relayed through the mates and deck officers. But the crew was too tired and beleaguered to complain or start trouble.

Barthel told himself, each time he saw misery and destruction, that the Obelisk's fall was Allah's method of testing the will of man. But the will of man was not giving an encouraging performance.

In their twenty-ninth day out of Golumbine the

ship-on-legs appeared. No action was taken. The *Trident* maintained her course and pushed northward, sailing more each day under the greenish light of the glowing patch in the sky. The pale luminosity, like light through thin clouds on a warm summer day, cast no shadows and did not glare from the sea or the ship's metal. Barthel was distinctly uneasy on deck facing that dismal, makeshift glow. Bar-Woten ignored it as much as possible.

But he didn't ignore the ship-on-legs. In the *Trident's* library he studied manuals on battle tactics at sea, more for his own peace of mind than any plan to pass on strategy. He knew that Prekari was well-versed in handling ships under dangerous conditions. But he had never been in a position to learn how wars were conducted at sea, and he found the difference fascinating.

The *Trident* wasn't equipped for a heavy sea battle. She carried only three guns, one fore, one aft, and one mounted midships, just aft of the first funnel. She also carried loads of split and dried logs to put into the burners for heat during a battle. In emergencies her methane tanks were always sealed and padded, and she either ran under sail or steamed on wood.

They were approaching the southern coast of Pallasta when the submarine appeared. Kiril had read about them, but it was a shock to see one surface and follow them two hundred meters astern, like a steel-clad whale. Prekari ordered gun crews ready and converted as quickly as possible from methane to wood. Smoke began to pour from the stacks. The stacks creaked and groaned, and deck officers supervised the loosening of the stack guy wires. The sails were

furled, and the *Trident* picked up speed, testing her
pursuer.

The submarine fell behind immediately and submerged. Prekari appeared on the quarterdeck walking
from side to side and peering over the railing. Not
knowing what else to do, he ordered sounding bobs to
be flung over the side all around the ship. Sailors
manned these and were instructed to report any less-
ening of tension on the ropes. If the submarine chose
to ram them from below, at least they'd know about
it. Bar-Woten thought it would be a useless advantage.
He stayed below with the engines, nursing a rod that
ran hot under the stress. His overalls were soon
soaked with hot grease. The smell of burnt packing
clogged his nose until he was sneezing every few seconds. But he refused to go topside. He refused to acknowledge he was being hunted by something he
couldn't see.

For seven hours they ran on alert. The sounding
bobs showed no change. Prekari stayed on the quarterdeck in a folding chair and ate his dinner in silence.
After finishing his last plate he wiped his mouth and
beard with a linen napkin and ordered the crew to
secure general quarters. They would continue to burn
wood until the next morning, but otherwise the ship
would run as usual until something new developed.

Bar-Woten went on deck as he finished his watch
and looked at the fire doves hovering over the pitchy
sea. The waters were less active with glowing sea life
now. Fish were seldom seen and seabirds were rare.

By the light of morning, gray and eerie, they saw
the coast of Pallasta. It was a savage, burnt ribbon of
black and brown. Weggismarche had had little peaceful commerce with Pallasta, a country more oriented

to military discipline and rigid political regimes. Up until four decades ago war had been almost continuous between them. It didn't look like there would be any more wars. Kiril looked up and down the ragged coast and wondered why God would allow such destruction, and for what purpose. His heart grew bitter and his nose filled with the acrid smell of singed land and dead waters.

By now it should have been winter in Weggismarche and Pallasta. But the air was warm and humid, and the few mountains they could see were rocky and snowless.

The ship-on-legs reappeared two weeks after its first reconnaissance. The *Trident's* crew watched it angrily, shouting and curling their hands into fists. Bar-Woten followed it with binoculars and noted it had guns on its deck. It rode with its hull out of water when it moved its fastest, but at other times it rode in the water like an ordinary ship, though still uncommonly fast.

Prekari kept the guns manned and put the ship under full alert again. He knew instinctively they would have to wait to be fired upon, if anyone was going to fire. The ship-on-legs had far more powerful weapons than the *Trident*. To provoke it would be insanity.

When the submarine surfaced in front of them, the crew shouted with rage and nearly went out of control. Prekari let them vent their feelings for a few minutes until they were hoarse and quiet, then ordered the sounding bobs to be set over the side again, though they could plainly see the sub ahead. The wood burners were stoked. The methane tanks were wrapped and secured with rubber-covered chains.

The submarine rose even higher in the water. A

hatch opened in its sail. A bearded man stood behind the hatch, using it for protection, and rested a bull horn on top. He addressed them in a language they didn't understand. When he got no response he tried again, and still they understood nothing. He shook his head and disappeared. Kiril, stiff with tension, stood on the bow holding his line and tried to sound out the phrases and riddle them. They were familiar, but he couldn't place them. He hadn't studied all the Obelisk languages, but he'd gone over enough of them to recognize many of the words.

Two men appeared behind the open hatch. One slipped and almost went off the ribbed decking on the back of the sub. He regained his footing and looked through binoculars at the *Trident*, paying special attention to the flags that fluttered from her rigging fore and aft. Then he said something to his companion, and again the bull horn was brought up. The man spoke Teutan this time, muffled and with a heavy accent, but recognizable.

"You are requested to follow us," he said. "You will be guided into port three days from here."

"That'll put us in the Pale Seas," Barthel told Kiril. Avra was beside him, her mouth set in a thin, grim line. Weggismarche sailors had always avoided the Pale Seas. Hegira, they said, did not behave there like it did everywhere else. At the terminus of the Pale Seas lay the Wall which determined the end of this section of the world. No one had ever been there and returned— not in recent memory, anyway. Legendary characters were said to have brought the stories back with them.

Prekari's answer came by messenger from the quarterdeck. The first mate read the reply through a hailing cone.

"We thankfully decline and request leave to follow our own course."

The ship-on-legs was drawing nearer. Signal flags were flying from its mast. Kiril couldn't read them, but Barthel could. He pieced them together. " 'Follow ship, or I will fire,' it says."

"There is no choice," the bull horn barked. "Follow or we will sink you."

Prekari kept his peace for fifteen minutes. Then he spoke, and the first mate hailed the sub again. "We will not allow a boarding party. We will follow you until fire dove Skhar reaches thirty-three degrees ascension. After that we will discuss the issue.

Barthel smiled. There was no fire dove called Skhar, and no bright ones that would reach precisely thirty-three degrees in these waters. The captain was using a delaying action.

"We do not understand the reference," the submarine said. "You will follow us, and there will be no further discussion."

Prekari gave the signal for all the guns to be loaded.

The ship-on-legs cut back its engines and fell slowly into the water, sliding behind the *Trident*. With the submarine in front and the ship-on-legs behind, there was little they could do. Prekari secured battle stations and ordered his mates to follow the submarine until further notice.

If they were heading into the Pale Seas, their course would have to take them past Pallasta's northern borders and Weggismarche. If there was nothing left in Weggismarche or Nin, then there was no reason why they shouldn't sail to the Wall itself. The first engine mate, a burly, hairy man, spoke to Bar-Woten as they watched from the poop deck.

"It's useless if we haven't got a home to come back to sometime or other," he said. He rolled his sleeves up and tied them with lengths of rope. "Let's go below and tend that rod. We're going to have to steam it up fine to follow that thing, and the captain's bound to keep us on wood. No chance to rest and switch over."

In and out, steam and water and heat coursed. It was the only life and hope Bar-Woten recognized. He imagined them captured by unknown men; killed, perhaps. The journey was now at an end as far as he could tell. He fell into a black funk and watched the rod smoulder, making mechanical movements to cool and relieve it.

17

The coast of Weggismarche was covered with falling snow. Ships passed them going in several directions up and down the coast, but none were from Pallasta or Weggismarche. All looked as though they came from the Pale Seas: fast, unknown, depressing. The air temperature was falling so rapidly that frost and sea ice formed on the deck and rigging. At the same time humidity increased until they were drifting through a freezing fog. All crew, on or off scheduled watches, worked to clear the deck and rigging of ice. Winter was coming late, but with a vengeance.

The fog obscured their view of most of Wiggismarche. Perversely, hope rose among the crew that somehow their country had been spared the worst destruction of the Fall; that they might slip away when the fog was thick enough and return to their home. It would be a long battle with these men from the Pale Seas, they said, but it would be better than not knowing—it would be better than dying in sight of the Wall where the world ended.

Prekari stayed isolated.

Kiril made sketches of the submarine and ship-on-legs whenever it was clear enough to see them. After a few hours of peering through thinning fog and straining his eyes in the murky light, he had enough details to piece together what he thought the ship-on-legs looked like from all sides.

It had at least four small guns on each side and two large ones fore and aft. Tubes were mounted along both sides, and banks of rectangular boxes squatted on the fantail. Dishes studded a mast rising from the bridge. It made a hideous roar when it was up to full speed and shot thin gray smoke from vents in the middle of the flat stern.

The submarine, what he could see of it, appeared to be fish-shaped like a tuna, with a thickened fin directly behind its head. This tower, or sail, was gunmetal gray. The back of the sub was decked with dark varnished wood.

The second day of their capture took them past the northernmost peninsula of Weggismarche where the Obelisk had once stood. It lay on its side spanning the isthmus like a bridge, buried in one mountain range on the peninsula and another on the continent, half its width lost in solid rock. It didn't appear broken as far as they could see, but the horizon swallowed its length in gray cloud. They passed the base of the Obelisk and saw it was smooth, as though cut by some unthinkable saw. The base thrust out beyond the mountain range of the peninsula and soared, a kilometer in the air, a square piece of chalk mounted on a rocky giant's ear. Where it had struck ground flows of molten rock had cooled into curled gray mounds, some reaching to the sea. All around was charred desolation. Kiril looked at it without any particular emotion. It was too incredible to believe. To him it seemed more likely the thing should have buried itself completely and been covered over.

He no longer thought of any Obelisk as a permanent feature of life on Hegira. The fallen spire was a monumental *thing*, like a stick thrust into an ant nest, its only purpose to stir up human lives. He loathed it and what it stood for—knowledge, gain, static civilizations, endless cyclopean achievement—all of it.

Hegira, too, had fallen in his eyes. The world was no longer self-evident axiom. It had to prove itself all over again before it could regain its solidity.

The submarine guided them into progressively shallower waters that changed color from deep blue-gray to gray-green. The waves took on a dismal milky sheen. The air became dry and very cold like a touch of dry ice. And nowhere, besides the ships that escorted them, did they see any signs of life. They were in the Pale Seas.

On the fourth day land appeared off the port bow. It was a narrow spit of sandy beach shrouded with thick ground fog. "It's embarrassed to show itself," Bar-Woten commented. It passed to stern by midday. Dusty green bushes dotted its northern slopes. By evening, on the starboard, sheer cliffs of reddish stone rose from the muddy sea. Birds wheeled around the waterline in white puffs. Their cries sounded like children mourning. A hooked and baited line dropped over the side brought up a small, almost featureless smeltlike fish, silvery when first pulled from the water, but milk white in death.

The submarine guided them into a barren, rocky harbor on the eighth day of their capture. They were ordered to drop anchor and await further instructions from the ship-on-legs, which was called a "hydrofoil." The submarine submerged and moved deeper into the harbor.

The captain ordered a sample taken from the water, and a cup was lowered over the side bringing up a liter of silty liquid. Prekari tentatively dipped his finger into it and tasted a drop. "It's not salty now," he said. "We're not in an ocean at all. We must be in a river."

Parts of the puzzle of the Pale Seas began to fall into place. From a few hundred kilometers north of Weggismarche on, the Pale Seas were actually one enormous river delta, which carried mud and silt from lands thousands of kilometers beyond. But the size of the river was staggering—where was its source? At the Wall of the World?

Barthel learned from Avra why few Weggismarche sailors had ever traveled into the Pale Seas, and none as far as they were now. He told Bar-Woten. Beyond the legends of unknown danger the Pale Seas were periodically flooded with a poisonous discharge, noxious gases rising from the effluent and discouraging passage. The peninsular Obelisk, it was assumed; marked a boundary line, since no other Obelisks could be seen to the north. What that implied, Barthel said, no one knew. But to the inhabitants of Weggismarche, Pallasta, and the lands around them, the north was obviously inhospitable. Yet now they had proof that people lived there.

The ship-on-legs hailed them by late afternoon and instructed them to weigh anchor. They were going to leave the harbor and sail against the current. Fortunately the wind would be with them.

By evening they saw smoke and haze. They pushed at full steam against the relentless water, sails taking a stiff breeze and masts and spars creaking with the strain. An unpleasant odor rose to greet them, subtler but more acrid than the single smell of the methane tanks. It stung the nostrils and made the eyes water.

From the distant shore, plumes of smoke rose from a colonnade of stacks. The air was filled with grease and soot. A brief, unpleasant thought occurred to Kiril—they were heading into hell, and fire and ice lay beyond.

The night was sleepless and unpleasant. As they lay at anchor in a small inlet, outside the swirling current, the darkness was filled with the roar of machines and the bellow of furnaces. The wind had dropped and now the smoke drifted thick about them, a foggy pall slowly closing in to suffocate. Barthel confessed he didn't like it at all. The trio met on the main deck at midnight and talked about what they'd do if they had to abandon ship. Barthel was reluctant to think about it; Kiril, on the other hand, was almost anxious. "I don't see any other chance," he said. "We'd be better off on our own now—"

"How's that?" Bar-Woten asked. "We don't know the local language, or what type of people live here, or anything we'd need to know if we wanted to slip by unnoticed. I'm frightened by these machines—I'll admit that and laugh at anyone who says he isn't."

"You've lost the spirit of the thing. We're supposed to proceed whenever possible," Kiril said.

The Ibisian examined Kiril in the dim glow of their covered lantern. The Mediwevan was staring into the dark.

"Not when we walk into an open fire instead of around it," Barthel said, shifting from his seat of ropes to the wooden deck. Kiril snorted.

"Listen," Bar-Woten hissed. "If this ship gets into a position no one can escape from, then we are trapped, too, and that's no good, I'll admit. We'll have to avoid that. But for the moment we can only wait and see. If the people who run the machines are as wise as they are clever, we may be better off than we think."

A whistle blasted beyond the hills surrounding the inlet. It sounded like a dying saurian. Kiril was sweating profusely, though the night air was almost freezing.

"So we do nothing," he said. "We sit and wait to die and give it all up."

The others said nothing. Bar-Woten turned to the glowing night air beyond the hills and licked his dry lips. He hated not knowing what there was to fight against.

18

The morning was obscured by fog. The *Trident* crew couldn't see any ships around her, or anything else. It would be a bad time to cut and run in unfamiliar territory. Most of her crew waited on deck for the fog to clear, talking and playing cards or resting quietly. Kiril wrote in a bound notebook he had bought from the ship's purser, who had a surplus of ledgers and logs. His entries were generally short, but this morning he was prolix. He stopped occasionally to put his pencil to the tip of his lower lip and reread his entry. He frowned. Then he set pencil to paper again and continued his pinched scrawl.

"How did you ever become a scrittori with handwriting like that?" Bar-Woten asked. Kiril looked up with a start at the Ibisian standing beside him and scowled fiercely.

"I'd like some privacy," he said, closing the book with a slap and putting the pencil behind his ear under a lock of hair. The Ibisian shrugged and started to walk away. Kiril looked distinctly miserable, then called for him. "I'm sorry," he said. "Come back and sit down." He patted the deck across from where he squatted. Bar-Woten returned just as stoically as he had left and sat. "We shouldn't fight all the time," Kiril said.

"No need for it," Bar-Woten agreed. "Not today, at least. We've chosen our fate."

"How's that?"

"We're going to run for it and follow the fog."

"How?"

"It will break with the wind and the wind is going south today, very gentle. We'll weigh anchor when we can see more to the north than to the south. The captain knows we have a clear channel directly east. We'll sound and follow the currents."

"But the submarine can see us whether there's fog or not."

"I don't see how," Bar-Woten said. "Water's silty."

"It must have some way. These ships don't sound as they sail; they just move."

"The submarine isn't here today anyway, unless it moved in during the night, and nobody heard anything. When the sub moves you can hear it in the hull."

Kiril shook his head dubiously and leaned against the back of a vent. "We won't get away that easily."

"We'll see."

They never had a chance to try their plan. Before the fog lifted the submarine was heard on the surface. When the fog thinned they saw two ships-on-legs moving too slowly to show their foils. Clusters of men in dark uniforms stood on the decks. A bull horn was brought out, and one of the men in black hailed the *Trident*.

"Captain Prekari!"

The captain came forward and answered the call. "I am Vice-Admiral Gyorgi Lassfal, in command of

Ocean Restoration. I was formerly in command of the Weggismarche Merchant Navy. Do you recognize my voice?"

Prekari, standing on the wing of the bridge, answered that he did not—further identification would be necessary. An exchange of personal pleasantries followed, which left no doubt in Prekari's mind that he was talking to his bureaucratic superior. He passed the word along the deck.

"Captain, I have been invited here to tell you there is no danger. These men wish us no harm. In fact they want our help in the Restoration. Am I allowed to board your ship and explain these things to you?"

Prekari told him he could come aboard alone.

The vice-admiral was brought to the lowered gangway by a small motor-launch that belched noxious smoke. He came aboard without ceremony and was ushered quickly into Prekari's stateroom. There was nothing left to do on deck but watch the rising fog and examine the near ships more closely.

By midday the vice-admiral left the *Trident*, and Prekari came back to the quarterdeck. He stood on the boat platform to tell them what had been decided.

"Weggismarche, Pallasta, and Nin are now under control of Northerners," he began. He cleared his throat and leaned on a davit. Bar-Woten thought of the day they had first met him, stomping along the deck to his cabin; now he looked tired and weak, half the man he had been. "That is, they are under the care of these people . . . who have lived in peace for many hundreds of years. The weapons and ships, they say, are defensive, used only when exploring in dangerous waters. I believe that story is true on the whole. So does Vice-Admiral Lassfal. They've come south to see what aid they can give to our country.

"They are building emergency shelters for the survivors. The factories we passed are for that purpose. The admiral claims they were brought here piece by piece in the last few weeks. They have ships much larger than any of ours. There are only five or six million people left in our country, a few more in the lands south. Most were killed when the Obelisk fell. All of our cities have been destroyed, the weather has been changed, the crops are all gone of course, and so is our livelihood. So far it sounds like they're benevolent, but I think they have other motives. Not unreasonable motives, mind you, but ulterior nonetheless. They have come to read the Obelisk. They have requested our help in digging out the buried portions—as much as possible—and reading and deciphering. The admiral tells me this is a monumental task, enough to fill decades, perhaps centuries. In that time the Northerners will support us, help rebuild, reestablish our economy—apparently making the Obelisk the center of all business and trade. They seem to be decent people—strong-willed, but not unreasonable. They have certain moral strictures we are requested to abide by. These will be outlined at a later date. There is nothing that should be repugnant to us. . . . " He didn't sound completely convinced. Kiril frowned. The captain's message seemed one of defeat somehow—defeat without war, without even preliminary defiance.

"The Obelisk is a thousand kilometers long. Until now we've never had a chance to read more than a few kilometers of its surface. We've known that the history of the First-born extended far higher, with

knowledge we could never hope to attain by ourselves. We are now offered the chance." He added in
a lower voice, "But at what a cost!" The crew of the
Trident was deathly still. The fog was gone now, and
they could smell the smoke from the factories.

"We have nothing else to do. We can't trade our
cargo, we can't buy necessary materials and parts, we
can't leave the Pale Seas and last for long with our
hearts cut out of us. We have to regrow our hearts
here, by giving up the sea, if need be, or working in
whatever way we can with this ship to help rebuild
Weggismarche. Of this I am convinced. Are you convinced with me?"

The crew said nothing. Then, as if by one motion,
they looked over the starboard side to the rugged and
denuded land and agreed in a low rumble. Kiril spoke
with them, and Barthel nodded with a catch in his
throat, mixed fear and sorrow.

Bar-Woten stood silent with his one eye fixed on
Prekari and his lips set. It would soon be time to begin the third leg of their journey.

From the top of Barometer Mountain, two kilometers above the barren plains that stretched to the Pale Seas, the long, geometric bulk of the Obelisk could be seen for at least four hundred kilometers. At the horizon half of its bulk was buried in the rock and soil of Hegira. Closer than that, the curve of the planet slacked away from the spire until its end spanned the isthmus of Weggismarche and wedged into another mountain four kilometers from Barometer. Kiril looked down the southern slope and saw the base camp of the surveying party from the *Trident*, and in the bay beyond, the *Trident* herself, tiny as a toy in a puddle. He turned his eyes skyward and shielded them. The light that had replaced the Obelisk's glow was at its noontime peak. Clouds drifted in patches across its concentrated center, casting broad shadows over Barometer and the bay. Bar-Woten climbed slowly and deliberately over the rock pile which edged the northern slope of the peak, and joined Kiril. Barthel wasn't far behind.

"I'm beginning to piece together this stuff about the Wall of the World," Bar-Woten said, regaining his breath with even, deep inhalations. "It's five thousand kilometers from here, to the north, which explains why there are no more Obelisks visible no matter how far north you travel. From what I understand the Wall itself gives off a glow at the top. There may be smaller Obelisks there or normal ones just beyond it."

"How tall is it?" Kiril asked. Barthel stood beside them and leaned on his climbing pick, his face red and sweaty.

"At least as tall as an Obelisk."

Kiril looked down the northern slope and saw a helicopter landing on a broad rock outcrop. It looked like a bee setting down on a stony gray flower. "Is it true there's writing on the Wall, too?"

"They say so. Because it starts at a forty-two-degree angle, they can climb up its face easier than any of us could scale an Obelisk. That's why they know more than we do. But they can't go higher than a hundred kilometers. The slope increases beyond that, and there's not enough air—not for a man or his machines anyway."

Kiril tried to picture the civilizations along the Wall developing faster, learning faster, and trying to spread their culture and knowledge farther south. How long ago had they reached the point where they could learn about submarines, hydrofoils, airplanes, and helicopters in sufficient detail to build them? A few centuries? How long after that before they could build rockets and read even more of the writing higher up? His past few weeks of education still stunned him.

There were huge factories farther north, whose only purpose was to create artificial petroleum products, following a formula on the Wall of the World. There was no natural petroleum on Hegira, as most half-civilized people had learned long ago. Some—such as those in Weggismarche and Pallasta, and even in Mediweva and Ibis—had developed efficient methane engines and made do with that. Those near the Wall, having access to more complicated instructions and designs and the method of making artificial petroleum from waste products, built their factories and developed engines with far more power, and also far more waste.

They had radio communication and were developing the transmission of moving pictures. They had basic rockets, though nowhere near as large as the one in the chasm south of Ubidharm. They had advanced medical knowledge. In all ways they were ahead of their southern neighbors. Yet they had been blocked by solid bands of ignorance, tribes and cities and countryside populations intent on stopping them from spreading Unholy Knowledge any farther. The People of the Wall had had to pass their information across the cultural interfaces gradually—over three hundred years' time—bringing their neighbors into their own fold. But even the People of the Wall had limitations—which began one hundred kilometers from the surface of Hegira.

Now with the fallen Obelisk there were no limitations. In a few decades they would be able to piece together the entire history, culture, and technology of all the civilizations of the First-born.

Kiril almost wished he could stay and learn. But it was too late to stop. The three had to pass beyond the Wall. It was a dead certainty that what lay beyond the Wall was the Land Where Night Is a River. He ran his hand across his forehead and smiled. It was like being halfway through a stormy day riding a scrittori balloon with clouds beginning to clear.

But they still had a long way to go.

"If we can't climb the thing, how do we get across?" he asked.

"I've been listening to their stories," Bar-Woten said. "Their legends seem to fit those of my country, end to end, completing the stories and adding more details. But they've also seen them—"

"Seen what?" Kiril asked.

"The holes. Every few kilometers there's a hole, about eight kilometers above the base of the wall." He was ebullient. He clasped his hands together and touched two fingers to his beard, smiling broadly as he looked across the plain. "They say when a man is worthy he can go into the hole and walk as far as he pleases . . . right across to the Land Where Night Is a River. Usually the holes are blocked—but for the worthy man they'll open right up!"

"And after that?"

"We'll see soon enough."

"Are they going to let us go north?"

"I don't know. We can only ask."

"They won't believe us."

"Probably not," Bar-Woten agreed. "So we don't tell them you're really a prince. We tell them you're a curious scrittori from a land they've never heard of, and we," he pointed to Barthel and himself, "are your humble student assistants. We've come to the ends of the world to see what there is to see and exchange what we have to give."

"You're hopelessly optimistic."

"These people have no reason to fight. No reason to conquer. They have everything already." He grinned. His guard's down, Kiril thought.

"I never thought an old soldier would trust anybody," he said.

"Nor I. That's why I left."

"The Bey trusts these Wall people?" Barthel asked.

"Why not? They could have killed us a dozen times over, and instead they ask us to join their work crews and help them restore a land they've never visited before."

"Maybe they're ambitious to a fault," Kiril suggested.

"What about the ship in Mur-es-Werd that was damaged by a hydrofoil?" Barthel asked.

"Ah!" Bar-Woten raised his hand. "One unanswered question. Maybe they fired first."

"Perhaps there's more than one civilization with technology like this," Kiril said. "What's going to happen when they all meet?"

"I don't know," Bar-Woten said. He stroked his beard nervously, then looked at Kiril as if the Mediwevan had pricked some happy private balloon and brought them all down hard. Kiril was surprised by the look—he'd made the suggestion almost cheerfully with the Ibisian's lightheartedness catching on. But he sobered and said, "That's the way it always is: two equals meet, and they have to fight it out."

"There is a reason for everything," Barthel said. "Allah dropped the Obelisk here to stop such squabbles. He dropped it in a land of good people perhaps."

"No, no," Bar-Woten mused. "Barthel, would your Allah sacrifice ninety million people to hand good cards and fair dice to someone else?"

Barthel frowned for a moment, then nodded, yes. "It would not be without precedent," he said. "My Allah is no simple God, Bey."

"I opt for letting the Fall remain a mystery until we hear a better explanation not based on faith," Kiril said. "There are things faith is good for, and this isn't one of them."

They scrambled down the southern slope toward the camp. A work party of fifty men and women were laying tarmac for an airfield a half kilometer from the beach. By the time the three had descended a whistle blew for dinner, and all work stopped.

A communal dining tent had been erected, and dinner was served inside with kerosene lamps on the tables. Most of the crew of the *Trident* was under the canvas, and about thirty People of the Wall, including the camp director. He was a grinning, gray-haired man, tall and slightly stoop-shouldered, who called himself Orshist. After the meal was finished he went to a small platform at one end of the tent and set up a board to outline the plans for the excavation of the Obelisk.

His manner was crisp and brief. He carried a collapsible pointer and used it to emphasize his words like a fencer executing a riposte.

"We have the spire," he said, "and we have Hegira. Hegira in this region has four layers that are familiar to us. They begin with topsoil, which is sparse here, and overburden, which consists of dead dirt and broken rock. Beneath that is the groundwater layer, which extends for at least a kilometer, and beneath that is plastic mantle. The spire has buried itself some four hundred kilometers from here, deep into the groundwater layer. Beyond that, at its midpoint, it has broken through this layer and struck mantle. But of primary interest is where it has lodged in the mountains. The mountains, contrary to what we've learned of geology on Earth, did not form because of drifting continents, of which Hegira has none. The mountains have always been here. Where the spire has fallen across mountains it has broken through four layers and found a fifth. This fifth is not another extension of mantle, but something quite different. It's porous like a honeycomb, made from what we now think is primary vulcanism—which could only have happened at Hegira's formation. Some of the pores are big enough for a man to step into."

Kiril and Barthel listened attentively, but Bar-Woten was mulling something over, his bearded chin resting in his hand. His eye was closed.

"If we wish to uncover the spire completely we must dig away all these layers where they cover the sides. We may never know all of the text on the underside, but fortunately the spire is unlike the Wall, and each side supports its own text instead of a continuation from side to side."

Bar-Woten opened his eye and thought of the honeycomb material, pores big enough to hold a man. That seemed very important, because it reminded him of the rind of a fruit they had eaten in Golumbine, called *sati*. It had a thin, tough outer shell under which was an equally tough but spongy and resilient white layer, like tree rubber. The white layer had been porous and dry.

Orshist went into detail about the excavations and produced a chart that showed where the first readings would be made.

"We have a pretty good idea of the history of the First-born to the middle of the twentieth century *anno Domini*," he said, pointing to the end of the Obelisk. "Information here could already give us a lifetime of study and development, since we come across complicated philosophies, whole new brands of physical science, and vast, important literatures. But now we need to know how we are related to the First-born and what sort of world Hegira is. With this knowledge we might begin to find some meaning in our existence."

Bar-Woten, like a weather vane, showed by the set of his mouth and the angle of his eyelid what he thought of Orshist's words. He didn't move a muscle otherwise. He reminded Kiril of a cat intent on its spring.

"So we'll begin in areas we can interpret. That will put us at this point, two hundred kilometers from the base. We'll also record at the very top of the spire, near the dormant sun source, but we won't begin direct interpretation. The language appears to be incomprehensible, even in the standard phonetic script of the spire. Numbers play a large part in the language toward that end. In short we are about to study the entire history and accomplishment of the First-born, perhaps up to the time they performed that unknown act, or had an unknown act performed upon them, and produced ourselves, the Second-born.

"Work crews will assemble tomorrow morning. Committees and working unions for the distribution of supplies and living quarters will meet and organize at each camp. Factories will be set up along the coast for the construction of roads, the rebuilding of cities, the manufacture of digging machines, and the processing of raw materials. We begin a job worthy of any civilization on Hegira!"

Kiril fidgeted. He could hardly remember what Elena looked like now, and yet he was still obligated—almost against his will—to push on with Bar-Woten and Barthel. He would rather have stayed and helped in the interpretation, in the learning and deciphering and recording, for the spirit of the thing was in his blood, and future adventure in unknown lands seemed far less attractive. His fists clenched, and he couldn't separate the confused strings of thought in his head.

20

"Kiril! Wake up!"

The Mediwevan fought out of his slumber and had the familiar sensation of not remembering where he was. The tent canvas overhead and the thin-padded cot, which had become as unyielding as stone during the night, had been forgotten in sleep, and now he didn't know what they were. Barthel came into the tent through the flap, stumbled over a roll of clothing, and grabbed him by the shoulder. Kiril rubbed his sleep-smeared eyes and asked what was going on.

"They arrested the Bey!"

"Who?" he asked, still foggy.

"The Bey! They've put Bar-Woten in jail!"

"Why would they do that?" he asked peevishly.

"I think," Barthel began, then lowered his voice, for others in the tent were waking, "I think he asked a woman to make love to him—solicitation, is that the word here? He was reported to some officials of the People of the Wall, and they put him in jail."

"Kristos," Kiril said, rolling his legs off the cot and plopping his bare feet onto the hard-packed dirt floor. It was cold. He searched hurriedly for his shoes.

"We should go to the captain," Barthel said. "He is

our representative until the new union leaders are voted for."

"I don't know," Kiril murmured, tying up his laces. He saw then that he didn't have his pants on, and it took him twice as long to slip them over his shoes and buckle the catch. He searched in the early morning grayness for his shirt and found it in the dirt, where Barthel's feet had kicked it off the roll.

The morning air was foggy and dismal. They walked across the rocky ground to the Administration Tent. No one was there yet, and the empty fold-out tables and chairs mocked them. The tent canvas flapped softly in the breeze. "Where's the jail?" Kiril asked. Barthel nodded and walked ahead of him across the fresh tarmac to the opposite end of the airfield, near the beach.

The jail was a wooden compound, which until now had been virtually empty. It was built of driftwood and tar paper and wasn't exceptionally strong, but its symbolism was still impressive. It was an ominous, ugly building, hodgepodge and scaly.

There was only one guard. He looked them over sleepily and then let them in. Bar-Woten was in a tiny cell faced with heavy iron-barred doors. He was wide awake and apparently hadn't slept all night. His face was an empty mask.

Kiril walked back and forth in front of the bars for a minute, fuming. "How in *hell* did you manage this?" he finally asked. Bar-Woten shook his head.

"I don't know," he said. "They're of your kind, not mine, I suspect. I had no idea a compliment to a woman was a crime."

"What an asinine thing to—" But Kiril cut himself off, looking at the jailor, and sat down on a small stool. Barthel remained standing, shifting from one foot to another. "What are we going to do?"

"Well," said Bar-Woten, switching abruptly from Teutan to Mediwevan, "we could take this as a warning and get the hell out of here, head north."

"What a mess that would land us in. How could we survive in this country?"

"You seemed anxious to try it a few weeks ago. It's either that or stand trial for something I'm obviously guilty of, with witnesses"— Kiril groaned—"and that would probably get me a year or so in prison. That's what this fine gentleman says," Bar-Woten grumbled, pointing to the jailer.

Kiril stood and told Bar-Woten they'd talk to Prekari. The Ibisian wasn't encouraged. "Listen," he said. "I sounded these people pretty carefully last night while I was being arrested. They have one fault, and it's similar to your own—they're self-righteous and highly moral on affairs of the flesh. They're peaceful and prosperous. They're also convinced they can fairly apply their law to all. Try overcoming that with the captain."

They left the jail and walked across the tarmac to the Administration Tent. There was activity inside—two young boys from the *Trident* were standing by the awning entrance with arms folded, radiating dignity, guardians of the ship's mates and the captain talking at a table within. Kiril and Barthel challenged the boys' bluff by walking in quickly and not saying a word until they were at the table. The captain stood up, tired and worn, and asked them what they wanted. Kiril told him what had happened.

"Serves the man right. Doesn't he have enough sense to be discreet?"

"I do not think discretion has much to do with it, sir," Barthel said. "I could have fallen into the same trouble. Any of your crew. Can we let him stand trial for a law we didn't know about?"

"It's a difficult problem," said a woman's voice from across the tent. It was Avra, sitting in a corner near the entrance with stacks of paper on a table before her. A shaft of light from a chink in the roof played about her hands, moving with the rippling of the tent fabric. Her face was dark and ghostly. She reminded Kiril of a Norn, and he felt a chill.

"What can we do about it?" he asked.

"Probably nothing. It's a minor charge and won't net him much of a sentence. He'll probably be taken to the settlement at the fifty-kilometer mark on the Obelisk, stand trial, and spend two or three months clearing dirt with the labor gangs. He can stand it."

Barthel spoke up, his voice surprisingly sharp, considering he was addressing Avra. "The Bey will not be locked up."

"He'll have to face it," Avra said tersely.

"You don't understand. He will kill somebody before that happens."

"Is he that stupid?" the captain asked.

Barthel pounded the table with his fist. His face was dark, and his eyes seemed clouded by smoke. "No one says the Bey is stupid!" he rasped. He turned and left the tent. Kiril stayed behind, uncertain what to do or how to interpret the scene. He felt he should apologize, but now he was angry, too. It seemed a ridiculous hindrance after they'd traveled so many thousands of kilometers and faced so much danger.

"We're their guests," Avra said. "We have difficult

diplomacies to work out with them, and very little to bargain with."

"The captain told us they were reasonable and helpful," Kiril said. "But all I see is smoke pouring into the Pale Seas and crews being set up to dig out the Obelisk. Now they slap us in the face with this ludicrous charge. I sense a darker motive."

The room was silent.

"No one behaves this way without a reason," Kiril added when the silence had lengthened.

"I think Barthel is right," he concluded, and he turned briskly to leave.

"All well, all good," Bar-Woten told them when they visited his cell for the second time. He hadn't moved. His body was charged with an electric tension. The guard—a man about Kiril's age—was pale and noticeably reluctant to stay in the building with him. Again they spoke in Mediwevan, but for a few moments Bar-Woten and Barthel conversed in Arbuck, which Kiril understood only slightly.

Then they left, and Barthel was quiet.

The day seemed unbearably long. Survey crews climbed Barometer and continued their measuring, but Kiril wasn't among them. He stood by the landing strip waiting for the plane to arrive, knowing it came this time to take Bar-Woten to his trial. He waited until dusk, walking to the food shed and mess tent after sunset to eat, then to the beach to listen to the swift surge of the river heading seaward.

The airplane didn't arrive by late evening, and the landing field, without lights as yet, was closed. Kiril went to his cabin to try for a few hours of sleep.

He didn't have a chance. He was caught between slumber and nervous alertness when Barthel called from outside the tent. The other sleepers grumbled, and one sat up in the murky light of the pole lamp rubbing his eyes. Kiril motioned for him to go back to sleep and held his fingers to his lips. Then he swung out of the cot, automatically picked up the clothes he had packed earlier, and left the tent.

A flaring gas flame provided a guttering illumination across the end of the camp, exaggerating the shadows and emphasizing the frequent gusts of wind. The night was dark and without bright fire doves. Barthel stood next to a barrel covered with a wire screen. Someone else was behind him, shadowy and indistinct, but Kiril knew who it was. "How did he get out?"

"Never mind that," Bar-Woten said from the darkness. Barthel took Kiril's arm and pulled him along.

They crossed the tarmac. Rocky and molten terrain began several hundred meters north of the camp. Bar-Woten told them they would follow the beach for a while, then duck into the stony maze if they were pursued.

"I thought there weren't supposed to be night landings," Barthel said. He stopped in the dark, squinting eastward. "They can't land on the runway. No lights."

"That's not an airplane," Kiril said. "It might be a helicopter. It's flying too low and too slow to be an—"

Bar-Woten grabbed both of them by the arms. "Quickly!" he said. "Into the rocks."

"Why?" Kiril asked, resisting the rush. "No one's after us."

"Trust a soldier's instincts for once! Into the rocks."

They broke into a run. Engines roared from the east. Bright lights split the camp into scattered spots of day. Barthel stumbled on a rock and split his knee

open. Limping and gasping, he held up his hands, and
they lifted him to cover behind the rocks. Kiril peered
over a split boulder and saw the base camp was alive
with running, shouting people.

"What's going on?" he asked wonderingly.

"They're being attacked," Bar-Woten said.

"Nobody's shooting—"

Gouts of flame billowed from the main tents. A
vivid red arrow of light swept the camp. Everything it
touched flared incandescent.

"They're ships," Bar-Woten said. "But they're going
faster than the hydrofoils—they're flying above the
water!"

At least five of the craft were approaching the
beach, each shooting lethal red beams into the camp.
The ships looked like broad scrub brushes scouring
the water. They danced on wide fringes of rubber and
threw plumes of spray behind them. Each was fifty or
sixty meters long, rounded and streamlined. They
didn't slow as they approached the beach.

Bar-Woten examined the Khemite's leg by match-
light. He tore a strip from the bottom of his shirt and
tied a bandage. "It's only a cut," he said. "Hold your
leg out straight."

"What are they doing up there? I can't see anything." Barthel gritted his teeth.

"They're killing everybody."

"Who? With what?"

"I don't know. Just be glad you're here."

"They're coming up on the beach!" Kiril said. "They
can go anywhere!"

"What are they shooting with?" Barthel asked.

"I don't know," Bar-Woten said. "Keep still."

"We have to leave, or they'll kill us too!" The Khemite groaned in pain.

"We're well hidden."

"They'll come after us," Kiril agreed. "God, I can't stand it!" he held his hands up to his ears. "It's slaughter!" He crouched to jump down from the ledge.

Something blinding flashed over them. His hair caught fire, and for an instant, amazed, he stood like a torch. Bar-Woten reached up and pulled him off the rock, smothering his head in a coat. When he removed the coat, the Mediwevan was unconscious. His scalp hadn't been burned, but the smell of singed hair added to the sickening smoke drifting across the rocks. Barthel's glancing eyes picked up stray gleams in the orange half-light. He struggled up from Bar-Woten's grip to look across the airfield. "Holy Allah!" he said, ducking down quickly. He grimaced as his knee flexed.

"Keep the leg straight!" Bar-Woten commanded.

"We can't stay here. We have to go farther away, or they'll kill us."

"You speak without thinking—" The Ibisian pulled his head in like a turtle as another beam flashed above them. "They've got the wrath of Samhain at work out there. They'll scythe us if we stick our heads up. Best to stay here for a moment."

There were fewer screams now. Scattered shots punctuated the crackle and hiss of burning. The engines of the craft throttled and hummed. Kiril came to and reached for his scalp. He brushed his hair vigorously with his fingers. They came away smudged. "Am I burned?" he asked.

"Not badly. You're lucky, young friend," Bar-Woten said. His face was fixed into a grim death's-head smile. Barthel leaned back in the shadow of the ledge and muttered prayers with his hands clasped. Kiril wondered why he wasn't praying himself. Mediweva's provincial God didn't seem to have any jurisdiction here. He brushed the singed hairs from his head.

"What are we going to do?"

"Wait," Bar-Woten said. He stood up and put his knees on the ledge, barely raising his head over the rim of the rock. "There are men leaving the ships. They've beached them, and the engines are off on three. They're carrying weapons—guns, I think. Some of the camp people are surrendering. They aren't shooting."

"Taking prisoners?" Barthel asked.

"It would seem so." He ducked back. "We'll lie low and creep around these rocks as fast as we can. Nobody is this close."

"Who are they?" Kiril asked.

The Ibisian shrugged. "The rivals are here. Do you think a bone as big as an Obelisk wouldn't draw every jackal in the area? The real story's barely begun now."

"Allah was good to us, having you arrested," Barthel said. "There is a reason for everything."

Bar-Woten grunted. "Let's go."

"Morning in an hour or so," Kiril said as they crawled over the rough, pebbly ground between the bigger boulders. "We should be pretty far from here by then."

An ear-pounding *whumpf* broke the quiet behind them. Bar-Woten stood up and saw the *Trident*'s fragments riding a flower of smoke and fire. Bits of blazing wood fell on the beach, forcing ranks of prisoners to break and run. "It's the ship," he said. "I don't think the new ones did it though."

"Did what?"

"She's gone."

They continued to crawl.

"Stop!"

Kiril looked up. A shadow on the rock above them pointed a gun into the crevice.

"Come out of there, all of you," the shadow said.

"What does he want?" Bar-Woten asked.

"He wants us to get up out of here," Kiril replied. "He's speaking English—good old King's English. That," he grimaced, "was my specialty a few years ago." He held up his hands, and the others mimicked him. "Coming," he said.

"Damn right you are. Nothing false, now."

A boat rowed silently near the water-washed rocks. It was filled with men dressed in black, all sporting wicked-looking rifles.

"Into the water," the man said. "It's shallow. Go on."

They were hauled into the boat and securely tied with scratchy ropes. Bound and helpless, they were pitched into the bottom. Someone came to stand above, bending with an odd profile and reaching out to examine them.

Barthel looked directly into the figure's face. His skin paled in the lamplight from the prow. Kiril lay face down in the boat and couldn't see.

"It's not a man," the Khemite whispered.

"Be gentle with these," the figure said, its voice muffled. "They're different from the others."

The oars were pulled in, and the boat drifted with the river currents.

21

Kiril looked their captors over quickly as they were shoved into line with the rest of the prisoners. The night hid the features of the one Barthel had said wasn't a man. It walked to the rear of the armed guards and whispered instructions to several uniformed men. It moved its limbs with an odd jerking motion, and its loose-fitting clothing formed novel humps and hollows as the wind grabbed at it.

Those tents that hadn't burned were being searched. Sporadic gunfire still accented the wind. The hulking flying ships whistled and hummed. A ramp was lowered from the nearest craft, and the first line of thirty prisoners was herded into a dark aft compartment, Kiril among them. Barthel and Bar-Woten were in the next line and didn't come aboard his craft.

The quarters were cramped and reeking with fear. A few lights flickered on above them, strips of white in the low ceiling, and they saw the floor was padded. Seats lined the walls. Those who could sit did so. Nobody from the *Trident* was in the group beside Kiril. He squatted on the padding and rubbed his face with his hands. His fingers came away wet with tears. He felt like dying, he was so confused.

The engines beneath them coughed, seemed to laugh, then broke into a body-strumming roar. The craft lurched and rose. The engines pitched higher.

Sometime in the next few hours he slept. He awoke in a press of bodies and struggled free of nightmares about slaughter. Most of the captives were breathing slowly, rhythmically, a sea of flesh gently rolling. He wiped sleep from his eyes and wet his finger to erase traces of dried tears from his cheeks. A few owlish eyes returned his gaze from across the room, but most of the prisoners were lost in blind, escapeful slumber.

He had to urinate. The pressure was almost unbearable. He crossed his legs and gritted his teeth to still the insistent acid pangs. There was already urine smell in the air from others. He felt a small, mild nausea, a reminder he still had a stomach and that he hadn't eaten for a while. At least the flying ship didn't roll with the water—if they were still over water.

He stood without disturbing those sprawled around him, stretched his arms, and tensed his leg muscles. He could touch the ceiling. With one finger he felt a light-strip. It was warm, but not hot. He thought of Barthel and Bar-Woten. Perhaps they were dead already, and he was on his own. He found that hard to accept. He had gotten so much strength from the two despite their differences.

"We've been moving for six hours," said a man across the cabin. Kiril recognized the guard of the makeshift jail. He had a broad bruise above his eye, and he held one arm as if it was a baby. "Did your friends get away?"

Kiril shook his head. Unsettled, he looked away from the guard. "Your friends didn't hurt me much," the man said. "But these bastards—I think they've broken my arm."

He didn't seem to hold a grudge, but Kiril still thought it best to consider everyone and everything an enemy now. He felt it was within his power to kill if he had to—something he had never known before. He flexed his hands and looked at them speculatively.

If Bar-Woten and Barthel were dead he'd have to protect himself. He was no longer a ward, an amateur. He was a caged animal.

The engines changed pitch. The craft banked forward, then rocked back. He tumbled over as they slowed.

The other prisoners were waking. Questions passed back and forth in volleys. A man and a woman hugged each other joyfully, then gazed around like cornered rabbits.

The engines stopped. The craft thumped gently to rest. The hatch opened and blinding daylight poured in, silhouetting five armed guards. The prisoners were herded from the craft down the ramp, stepping into soft snow covering gray concrete. Slate-gray mountains rose on three sides, and on the fourth a stretch of wave-flaked water. Above was a bank of rushing clouds, piling around the mountains and sculpting wind-saucers in their lee. Kiril's heart leaped with the crisp smell of the air—forests and cold stretches of beach, lakewater smell, rain smell. The land was horrible and beautiful at the same time, the mountains raw with black jagged rock and stunted trees, the wind like a flight of icicles. The prisoners beat themselves with their arms and puffed their cheeks out, huffing, trying to keep warm. The guards kept their slender guns raised and ready.

The thirty were lined up on the concrete and snow in two rows and made to stand until they were blue.

A second craft climbed from the water of the lake and whisked across the concrete apron to park beside the first. A third followed, and both disgorged loads of prisoners. These were lined up twenty meters behind Kiril's row. He craned his neck searching for Bar-Woten and Barthel. He thought he saw the Khemite, but couldn't be sure. He was afraid to turn. His teeth chattered until they threatened to vibrate his aching eyes out. His ears were numb, and when he touched his armpit-warmed fingers to them, they tingled.

Trucks with canvas-covered beds rolled onto the strip and stood with engines idling, white smoke belching from pipes hung near the cabs. Kiril saw the shrouded figure climb down a ladder from the second hovercraft. It wore a silvery mask beneath its dark hood. Two men conferred with it, then took its arms and led it to the cab of the truck. It tugged them to a stop and turned to point to the ranks of prisoners. Its hand, Kiril saw, was gloved. Beneath the silvery mesh of the glove there could only have been three fingers, unless more than one digit occupied each finger. He felt a tremor pass through him that was more than just cold. Where could such a thing have come from? Perhaps, he consoled himself, it was only a man made up to look strange to cow the captives. But its walk was so authentically different that he doubted it was human.

The guards prodded the captives with their guns and marched them into the backs of the trucks. There in the windy canvas tunnels they sat until the gates were closed and the trucks lurched ahead. Then they rushed to peer out the openings between the truck panels and the canvas.

Kiril found a position where he could see the concrete landing field pass beneath them, changing to a rocky, ice-pocketed road.

"We're being guarded from the cab," word passed. "They have guns aimed on us."

"Maybe we can slip out the rear," a woman suggested. She stood up to see if the folds of canvas above the gate were tied down, but was wrenched back into her seat by a sudden bump.

"We're going too fast," a man said. "We'd be killed."

"We're going to be killed anyway," the jail guard said. "You know who these people are? They're from the *east* . . ." He said the word as if it were synonymous with evil.

"We don't know that yet," another said.

"Who else could build machines like these but the ones who've been dropping rockets on the Library Cities?"

"There may be others, but even so, they're all trying to destroy us," the woman near the gate spoke up. "We have to get away from them and fight!"

Kiril listened with interest. "Two equals," he murmured to himself. "They have to fight it out."

But it wasn't only their fight. With instruments like the fire guns and flying ships it wouldn't be long before everyone on Hegira would face a rout. It would be Bar-Woten's March all over again—but this time the Ibisians would look like reckless children.

He remembered the Bible and thought of Cain and Abel. Cain meant "smithy," or forger of tools. The tool-forger slew his farmer brother because God looked on the brother's sacrifice with more favor.

Now in a different place and far different time, those
with the better tools won—just as the tiger with the
swifter claws gained dominance in the forest. Mercy,
kindness, grace, and beauty had nothing to do with
human existence in such crazed times. He shook his
head. He was so far from all of it, so isolated in mind
and temper—yet he dearly wished, with a portion of
his darker soul, that he had the finest tools of all. He
would scourge his way to the Wall like a tide of cats
through a mouse village—a tide of stray cats. All the
stray cats were licking at him, testing him with claws,
pulling away the pieces of soggy paper he had wrapped
around himself for warmth. They mewed and purred
and rubbed against him—

He lifted his head up and wrapped his arms around
himself to stop his shivering. He was freezing—they all
were. More and more quiet, eyes glazed, faces blue,
lips purple. The truck jolted to a stop.

Hardly aware where he was going, Kiril followed
the stumbling crowd of prisoners down a sloping
ramp into a concrete corridor. The guards jostled the
slow ones until they regained their footing and
lurched after. Kiril's feet were numbed stumps.

But it was warm! Warm air flowed up to meet them
as an inner door opened, and they leaned into the re-
vivifying breeze as if it were life itself. Moaning,
crying, and grunting with pain, they were pushed into
a narrow, gray-green waiting room. Kiril felt his pants
crackle, then go damp. He had urinated, and the urine
had frozen on his trouser legs. He didn't care.

He thumped himself and grinned and kicked his
legs out, as the others did. But in a few minutes their
joy turned to misery. Their limbs began to thaw, and
with each inroad of warmth a rigid needle poked at

their bones. Then their muscles cramped and they cried out in agony.

Other prisoners followed. Barthel came through the door, his face haggard and pale olive, and behind him a man with a patch. They were both alive! Kiril felt like shouting at them, but his tongue cloyed his words. He was filled with a deadly thirst.

He had never been more miserable in all his life. But each little addition of misery, which in itself would have made him weak and ill, seemed to diminish the total. He seemed to draw strength from his pain and discomfort.

The groups weren't allowed to mingle. They were pushed up against the opposite walls and told to flatten themselves or lose their legs. Iron bars swung from the ceiling and enclosed them, giving just enough room to stand flat to the wall. They could only look across at their caged companions. Bar-Woten reached his hand out to Kiril and feebly gestured. A guard butted it with his rifle.

Hoses full of lukewarm water were turned on them. The air was filled with steam as the water sprayed against the cold walls. Blood, dirt, urine, and feces washed from the prisoners and whirled away down the drains in the middle of the room.

Kiril guessed there were about a hundred of them. They were shivering again in the wet and screaming with the pain of their thaw. Kiril suddenly found himself elevated to a level of calm detachment. He looked on the prisoners and their captors and saw only silly, inconsequential animals. Then what was he? Another animal, temporarily jolted above concern with his body, perhaps to share some higher sense of humor.

They all looked ridiculous—playacting amateur roles conjured by ridiculously limited talents.

Could he think of anything better? No, he admitted. He was no better. Just less blind.

A second spray, pungent with disinfectant, was directed over them. Fans and radiant heaters were brought in from another door. The heaters were turned on, then the fans.

When it was over a third of them were dead. Kiril dragged himself out of a swimming haze and looked at the middle of the room. The cloaked figure was standing there talking to a uniformed man. The man's face held a mixture of obedience and repugnance. The ends of his mouth curled downward in a half-sneer, half-snarl. He said something Kiril couldn't hear.

The figure gestured with a draped arm, and the fans and heaters were carried out. The officer walked before the opposite row of prisoners, glancing diffidently at the hanging corpses. He spoke, first in the melodic tongue of the People of the Wall, then in loud, clear Teutan.

"Some of you here may be important to us."

"I am!" a man shouted. "I'll talk about anything!"

The officer's look changed to scorn. "You'll be asked questions. They require specific answers, correct answers." The officer smiled. "If you don't answer correctly, this man is a demon. You've noticed his shape? He comes from hell, not a woman's womb. He'll broil your hearts as if they were on a spit. I hope you understand."

The cloaked figure turned to the wall opposite Kiril and began at one end. Its sibilant voice reached through the sudden quiet like a serpent's hiss.

Kiril struggled to stay aware, but he couldn't. His

vision narrowed. He looked at everything through a wind-filled cave, drawing farther back with each second until the rush carried him from the receding light.

"And you," the voice asked. "You are from very far, too, are you?"

Kiril looked up. He wiped a dribble of saliva from his lower jaw as he stared into the silvery mask. "Elena," he said softly.

"How far away do you live?"

"Mediweva," he answered. "Very far."

"Just a sailor who's traveled far? Or did something compel you to come here?"

"Something," Kiril said. "Elena. Take off your mask."

"What brought you here?"

"You did."

"Not I. Something specific."

Kiril saw Barthel and Bar-Woten standing in the middle of the room under close watch by three guards.

"I had to save you. Save her." He was aware now whom he was talking to.

"Her?"

"My only love." That was hypocritical, he thought. The self-accusation echoed and vanished.

"Ah." The figure gestured.

The cage opened. When he fell, he was caught by yielding arms and taken to join his companions.

"Did you see where we are?" Bar-Woten asked. A guard shouted at him. He glared back. "We're in the country of the Wall!"

The guard raised his rifle, and Bar-Woten backed off with hands up, placating.

The Wall.

22

They sat in the tiny cell and stared listlessly at the padded walls. Bar-Woten crouched with his hands clasped between his knees, knocking his knuckles against his legs. Barthel stood and picked his teeth with a fingernail. They had been given a thick gruel three hours before. It was acting on them unpleasantly. Kiril lay on his back with head and shoulders leaned against a wall, looking green and feeling very docile.

"We've been drugged," Bar-Woten said. Kiril nodded. They wouldn't offer much resistance in their condition. A small window in the door showed them the hall outside, and by peering at an angle they could see the rigid shoulder of a guard, but nothing more.

The door swung open. An officer stepped into the cell and looked down at Kiril. "You are the Mediwevan?" he asked in thickly accented Teutan.

"Speak English. I can understand. Yes, I'm the Mediwevan."

"Come with me," the officer said. He reached down and picked Kiril up. With a last look over his shoulder at his companions he was pulled down the hall to a brightly lit room beyond.

The room was outfitted like a surgery ward with a central couch covered by worn brown leather and strips of absorbent cotton. He was strapped onto this and his pulse and blood pressure were taken. An orange-robed man with intersecting black lines drawn across his bald scalp bent over him with a syringe in hand.

The demon-figure entered from another door. "You may administer," it said. It leaned over Kiril as the needle went into his arm. "This will not hurt you. Just to find out what you know . . ."

Kiril went blank.

He awoke with a sour taste in his mouth and the shock of smelling salts in his nose.

"You've been very cooperative," the thing in black told him. He was taken to the cell. Barthel and Bar-Woten were removed next. Kiril asked the guard why they were both going. The guard looked at him sternly, then checked up and down the corridor before answering. "We're pretty sure you're the one we want," he said. "But we will test these two just in case." He swung the door shut and locked it.

In two hours the Ibisian and the Khemite were brought back. Bar-Woten weaved a little and slumped to the floor. Barthel stood rigid against the wall, eyes wide and staring into the opposite corner of the cell.

"What did they make me say?" Bar-Woten asked.

"Nothing," Barthel snapped. The Khemite looked into the corner and flinched as if from a blow. What Bar-Woten had revealed under hypnosis was slowly mangling Barthel's insides. He had never suspected. . . .

Overhead they heard the sounds of distant explosions. Kiril peered through the window and saw the guard standing away from the cell, looking anxiously down the hall.

The lights went out. After an hour they slept. Bar-Woten snored loudly, head lolling between his legs. Kiril hung on the edge of sleep. He heard someone move in the cell, but stirred and drifted off.

"No," Barthel said. He closed his eyes but couldn't block out what he saw. In the corner, standing above the reclining Kiril, was Barthel's mother. She glowed faintly like the sea, and her throat opened into a second smiling mouth. What she murmured to him he could not accept. But it was true. He had heard. "Not now," he said.

She spoke to him again.

"No."

He turned away from the corner and butted his head softly against the padding.

The lights came on again. Kiril stood and stretched in the cramped space. Barthel slept on, standing with his head wedged into the corner. Bar-Woten looked at Kiril speculatively from his spot on the floor.

"You're the chosen one," he said. "They're sure you're the one who'll get them into the Wall."

"Get who in?"

"The thin ones. You told the right story, I suppose. Barthel didn't. I'm sure I didn't. The one who isn't human, it spoke to the guard while they were making Barthel talk. It spoke English but I could understand. There are three of them here."

"Three of who?" Kiril asked, mind still foggy from sleep.

"The thin, strange ones. They aren't from this part of Hegira. They came across the Wall in a ship of some sort. They've made a pact, and they're sharing knowledge with the English-speakers."

"They want me to take them to the Wall?"

"You're lucky," Bar-Woten said, nodding. "You'll reach your goal. I doubt if we will."

"I don't want to help them with anything," Kiril said. "They don't deserve it."

"The thin ones might be more friendly than the English-speakers. They didn't like the slaughter at the Obelisk camp. Seemed to think there might have been more like you. Dead pilgrims are no good to them."

"What are the English-speakers doing for them?"

"Didn't say." Bar-Woten's face crinkled into a smile. "It's fairly obvious, though. The thin ones want to get back to where they came from."

"Through the Wall?"

"Any way they can. Perhaps the English-speakers are building them another rocket."

"Then I pity them. They'll be double-crossed."

Bar-Woten shrugged. "I don't understand much of anything now."

Barthel jerked and pulled away from his corner. He rubbed his eyes, then looked over Kiril's shoulder and seemed relieved.

The door opened an hour after they were all awake. Another officer, paunchy and florid, ordered them out of the cell and took them down the hall in the direction opposite the laboratory. Two young, wan-faced guards followed with holstered pistols.

A hovercraft waited on the concrete airstrip. Craters ten and twenty meters across had been punched into the pavement and the surrounding rocky hills. Fragments of metal littered the area.

The fat officer rapped the butt of his gun on the

port of the hovercraft. The port swung open, and a ladder came down. "Climb in," he told them. They went up the ladder into the ship. The guards followed, and the officer managed to squeeze through with some straining. A low, round metal tube led them around the circumference to the main cabin. A small barred cell had been welded to the floor and ceiling of the adjacent passenger cubicle. The guards put them in and locked the door behind.

The hovercraft coughed and roared. Somewhere metal screeched across concrete. Then she lurched and rose. The pilot, hidden behind a thick steel shield, took them across the apron and over the lake.

They could get glimpses of their flight only through the edges of the clear canopy that extended beyond the shield. Gray, cragged mountains came toward them as they skirted the perimeter of the lake. The rocks passed away abruptly as the hovercraft made a long, slow turn to the right toward the middle of the lake. Rock walls flashed by on both sides as they passed through a narrow sound.

Barthel stared with determination through the bars at the shield. Bar-Woten sat relaxed with his back wedged into one corner of the cell, studying the slender view of their travel. Kiril alternated between his two companions and the view, trying to puzzle what had happened to all of them.

The trip took an hour. The hovercraft slowed and pulled into a narrow harbor ringed with walls of slate-black stone. It vaulted with a rumble and a slight bump up a ramp of wooden pilings. The guards came alert suddenly and opened the cell on orders from the fat officer. They were led outside.

"We have a special treat," the officer said, slipping

the words conspiratorially from the side of his mouth as they walked beside him. "A parade. You should enjoy tomorrow."

Ahead of them lay a solid mass of grayness, like concentrated storms packed so thickly they merged without feature. Nearer, clouds broke from the monotony and asserted their own turmoil. Rain fell in windblown draperies onto the green, jungle-covered hills and valleys that butted up against the ascending curve of the Wall. Nearer still, obscured by plummets and feathers of mist pouring over the hills, were masses of buildings, angular, like scattered blocks of lead. The sight made Kiril's heart sink. A land of no cheer, no variety . . . it choked the eyes. Yet it had an unmistakable, grave grandeur.

The officer was obviously proud of his city. But he was also a little cowed, as though the solemnity and monotony were not exactly what he'd expected. Thunder pranced near the gray end of the world. The Wall flashed sheet-white with an eyelike wink—roof of clouds the upper lid, gray-green jungled hills and peaks the lower. The gaze was cold and expectant, like the eye of an *untersay draken*.

"Faster," the officer said. The wind picked up and ruffled their matted hair.

A long, sleek silver train waited for them at the end of the wood ramp. Steam hissed from the engine. The rails made plaintive squeaks. The air smelled of lightning and storm. It tickled Bar-Woten's nose, and he wriggled his face, making his patch bob. He threw a side look at Kiril as he rubbed his nose. Clearer than anything, it told Kiril the Ibisian was worried.

"This car," the officer directed. They climbed into the stepwell, then waited as the inner door opened.

More guards waited within, and two of the hooded thin ones. The interior of the car was dark brown suede and chrome steel with a cleanliness that showed rigid care. Two olive-colored tanks of translucent glass were bolted to the floor at the opposite end of the car. The older, tougher guards around these were fully armed. They carried pistols, daggers on their belts, and heavy, brutal rifles stubby as toadstools.

The three were forced to sit in a single seat with prods of elbows and hands on shoulders. The thin aliens stood immobile and silent a few steps from their tanks. Thick fluid lapped in the cylinders. An array of pipes curved from each tank and disappeared into the floor.

The train began to move.

The greater part of the ten-minute ride was spent on a long, fragile-looking trestle that crossed over labyrinthine ridges of jungle-covered rock. Rivers crept through the gorges and poured into the lakes farther south, eventually falling into the Pale Seas. The ridges began to look artificially flattened, though still verdant; then buildings occupied them, and finally the land rose in one triumphant, humorless surge to a series of plateaus. The city of the English-speakers sprawled across the tablelands. Closer, the buildings glittered with walls of glass and polished metal. Counterpoints of coppery red and rust lanced up the sides of the taller structures. Monumental cubes were rolled on edge and supported by concrete pillars, faced with glass and steel and something the color of pewter. There were towers, prisms, all sharply sketched, all flat planes and daggers. Every mesa's cluster was tuned to emphasize the highest, central plateau, which met the Wall. Here the buildings resembled crystals of chrysolite and spar, featureless at this distance, divided by walls of deep jade green. The train worked steadily over and between the mesas, rising slowly, crossing trestles when valleys intervened, surrounded by walled throughways on the tablelands. It was an armored, protected millipede crawling laboriously to meet the cloud-worshipped Wall.

Kiril was too dazed to be impressed. The scene rolled by with a featureless, chaotic irregularity. It was meaningless because it was unlike anything he'd ever seen before. Later, perhaps, he might have nightmares about it, but now he could not assimilate. He could only stiffly wait.

Barthel saw nothing but an empty seat on the opposite side of the car. His lips worked.

The highest plateau was breached. The millipede slowed and chuffed, then coasted smoothly into a ceramic-lined tunnel. Daylight flashed as it left the tunnel and sidled against a slant-walled building.

They were taken from the car. The entourage of guards and officers in the car surrounded the three foreigners and two nonhumans as if they were some treasure to be protected.

Again, in the interior of the dull, gold ziggurat, they were fed into a cell more spacious and comfortable, but still with the door locked and the walls padded. They were not searched. They'd been closely watched.

Barthel, however, had kept himself immobile throughout the journey. He had been ignored for long moments. No one had noticed his hand reaching down to break off a strip of metal edging the seat. Not even Bar-Woten had seen it.

Only the woman in the seat opposite. She had smiled.

23

Hours passed. The cell was darkened, and they lay on their cots waiting. Kiril heard Bar-Woten snore. He squeezed his eyes tightly shut. He tried to remember Mediweva. Somehow he found his way there, and his body relaxed.

Something moved in the dark.

Barthel was wide awake. He reached under his shirt and felt for the sharp strip he had pried loose in the train.

She was glowing, and both mouths moved. Numb, he swung his feet out over the bed.

The Bey had said startling things. He had said things that fifteen years of travel together had never revealed—could never have revealed. In saying them he had raised the past, brought it back to haunt Barthel with all the things he knew would be best left forgotten. Dropped like plum stones in a pond.

Bar-Woten stirred in the dark and murmured.

The ghost told her son he was no longer Barthel, servant to Bar-Woten. Your name is Amma bin Akka. You are free. Enact your freedom.

Kiril heard a shout and the tearing of fabric. He sat up half-awake and grunted a question.

Bar-Woten felt the resistance of the flesh and the

warmth of the blood, and then it was too late. He had reacted with all the automatism of a scorpion's tail sent clicking to its prey, had avoided the knife, not thinking who was attacking, had thrown up the bed-clothes and entangled the shadow with them; and the shadow had struck out with the metal, flailing like an enraged child with its fist, shrieking hoarse and kicking. Knowing with twenty years of war experience behind him where the blade was, Bar-Woten had plucked the hand from dark air and turned the blade inward and driven it home; not a chance, the attacker had no chance and perhaps had known that; but with a gasp he went down, and whether there had been blood first, or the resistance of the flesh, or the tearing of the cloth, there was no knowing. It was all muddled.

The light came on. A guard stood sleepily in the doorway.

"They were going to kill you!" Bar-Woten said, seeing Barthel on the floor, blood welling from his stomach. "They were going to cut your throat just like they did your sisters', rather than let us take you alive!" His voice was a whisper, soft and wondering. "We killed them to keep the rest of you alive. I've never—"

He brought the strip up to look at it.

The guard shot him twice through the head.

24

The aliens walked behind Kiril. To all sides of them
armed guards formed a phalanx. The procession
moved through the high-walled canyon of steel, glass,
and concrete. They were watched by hundreds of
thousands of people who sat on the tiers on each side
of the boulevard. Paper streamers sizzled through the
air and confetti fell in hard, itching flakes. Vaguely
Kiril heard the carnival cheers and the cries of "Pilgrim! Pilgrim! Find your way!"

Amplifiers high above churned out a tinny refrain:

> "Find your way, make love to the Wall,
> Be the clown who will learn,
> The fool who might return. . . ."

He couldn't make out the rest. It was a mummer's
farce, and he was the central caricature, a lone, un-
spectacular man who had come tens of thousands of
kilometers to be paraded up the street of the sophisti-
cated English-speakers, to be met with ridicule and
ceremony, then sent to the Wall like a belled goat.

He hated them fiercely. He saw in them all the concentrated pus and useless decay of the Second-born.

He hated himself. He had survived. That incomprehensible decline and violence that had ended the journey of his companions hung like a dead weight from his feet and slowed his walk. Guards pushed him on.

Only two of the thin ones accompanied him. The third was staying behind as part of the agreement. The others would climb the eight kilometers up the slope with him.

The street ended at the Wall. He was handed a pack full of food and climbing equipment. The aliens were given steel cylinders and cloth-wrapped parcels. Behind, the noise of the crowd subsided.

"This is not our doing, human," the alien in dark green told him as they started to climb. "We have a journey as you do. May we all succeed."

Kiril nodded automatically. He was the thousandth pilgrim to be sent up the Wall in a fool's parade. The last had been a year ago before the arrival of the thin ones.

"Why don't they just kill pilgrims and be done with it?" he asked.

"They cannot stop them. Once pilgrims came from their own people; they cannot deny the motivation that guides them up the Wall. It is a matter of public record. Nor can they deny what happens when pilgrims return."

"Some have returned?"

The figure in green was silent for a moment. The second, dressed in black, stopped climbing and pointed its silvery mask at Kiril. A thin whining sound came from under the cloak.

"There have been no pilgrims from this land for ten years," the first continued. "The migrations began only twenty years ago. But we have learned. At other places and along other points of the wall the streams of pilgrims have increased a thousand-fold in the last few months. Some cities are inundated since the fall of the Spire. They are all motivated by one thing—that which we drew from your memory—the loss of a mate. There are females as well as males."

"Why is it happening?"

The enigmatic silver mask was silent again.

"Don't you know?"

"We don't," the figure in black said. "They migrate to appease"— again the whine—"a fairy tale. Most are killed on the journey. Most are already dust or mud. But you survived."

"Not without help. I owe my life many times over—" He cut himself off and shook his head.

"No one will ever understand your people, or ours," the first said.

"I intend to try," Kiril concluded.

Eight kilometers up the Wall there would be a circular entrance. The hole, ten meters across and fifty deep, would end at a blank barrier. If he was worthy the barrier would open to him. If not he would probably die trying to get back down the slope, too demoralized to be careful. Either way the English-speakers would never see him again.

The clouds bathed them in cold, neutral wafts.

Kiril pried more information from them as they climbed. He learned that Obelisks were falling every thirty thousand kilometers, the nearest to them being the Obelisk in Weggismarche, with enormous destruction of life. But people returning to the stripped land were now able to view most of the Obelisk texts. That meant soon most of the people of Hegira would know, or be forced to know, the history and accomplishments of the First-born. Then they would have to accept what they were.

He didn't think of Elena or of Bar-Woten or Barthel. He thought only of the climb, aching thighs and calves and arms and neck stiff from the cold and looking up. This was the last step of the migrating worm, he told himself. God's gaze was not intense light, as he had been taught by the Franciscans, but cold dank cloud and tears.

The Wall cried. Its condensation ran to the land and formed rivers. It made the footing slippery, like walking up the side of a wet glass—but there was always the traction of the engraved words.

The thin ones climbed steadily, tirelessly, with a wobbling gait, arms reaching out to steady themselves, their suit-wrapped, cloth-covered bird legs pumping.

"Why did you come here?" he asked as they rested.

"We are not sure you would understand, human," the figure in green said. "But you might. We wish to know what happened to us. Long ago all was bliss and paradise, and we grew. We were all part of . . ." It whined sharply. "A reach. We reached a peak of achievement and understanding. Then it was all lost, and we had to start from the beginning with hurt and the disaster of youth. It is not precisely the same with you."

"But not terribly different," Kiril said.

"Perhaps."

"Are they going to help you get back if I don't?" He motioned to the fog-hidden city below.

"We are exchanging help for knowledge, yes."

"You know what they'll do with that knowledge," Kiril said. The thin ones didn't answer.

Four kilometers. He hooked his sleeping pouch into the words with a net of tiny grapples and rested for the night. The thin ones had their own apparatus. They slung themselves from similar grapples and replenished something in their suits from the steel cylinders. Kiril did not sleep well.

With green morning they fought their way through clouds like ghosts of trees. Five kilometers. Six.

"There is the entrance," the figure in black said. They automatically picked up their pace, though Kiril was exhausted.

They rested at seven kilometers, and the fog obscured the hole again.

The next day they entered the Wall.

"There is no barrier," the green-cloaked one said. "You have made it, pilgrim."

A tunnel without end led deep into the Wall, filled with warm, dry luminescence. Kiril tossed aside his climbing tools and most of the contents of his pack, then squatted near the edge and examined the tunnel closely.

"We would like you to proceed," they told him, waiting.

He got to his feet, picked up the almost empty pack, and began walking. He paid no attention to the nonhumans behind him. After a half hour he stopped and looked over his shoulder to see what they were doing.

The tunnel had been sealed behind him. He couldn't see either of them. They hadn't qualified. He shrugged and continued his hike. Ahead, he knew, lay the Land Where Night Is a River.

He ate and slept.

Then he walked again. Before his next sleep he

walked ten or eleven kilometers—or as much as fifteen, there was no way of telling—and still the tunnel was featureless.

But in the next kilometer he came up against a blank barrier. He paced back and forth in front of it for an hour, sweat beading on his face and darkening his shirt. He was furious and he reached out to strike it with his fist. His hand vanished, and he stumbled through the barrier.

At that moment he began to understand the power of Hegira. Beyond the insubstantial partition was a clear view of darkness and fire doves. He stood in a broad glass hemisphere. The air was musty, but breathable. A waist-high wall surrounded the base of the dome. He walked to the edge and looked across the top of the Wall. It was a featureless dark plain that stretched as far as any horizon on Hegira's lower surface.

On the other side of the dome he looked down through clouds and atmosphere to the surface of his world. He traced the rivers and mountain ranges and the broad delta of the Pale Seas. He could see the cloud-wrapped line of the fallen Obelisk in Weggismarche and Pallasta and the upright Obelisks of other lands. For hours he stared at the umbers and greens and grays of land and forest—the russets, siennas, and ochers of deserts and plains, the tracks of mountains like frost on glass and the puffs, fish bones, and anvils of clouds, storms, and hurricanes, stretching to a broad line of blue at the horizon—and rising above them all, the stolid needles with their tops of sheet-sunlight.

Then the Obelisk light faded. The land became shadowy. Night snugged fit across Hegira. The fire doves gleamed more brightly without the competition of daylight.

With a contentment he hadn't known since childhood—a deep recognition of forces higher than himself in which he could trust, for they were looking after him—he put his gear on the floor of the dome and went to sleep beneath the inconstant glimmer of the fire doves.

He awoke from some vague dream and rolled over onto his back. "Good morning," the man standing over him said. Kiril tensed and slowly backed out of his wrappings. The man was dressed in clothes similar to his own, carrying a duplicate pack. His face was well tanned and lined with wind-wrinkles, and his hair was a backward-sweeping mop of gray. His nose had been broken numerous times, and his lip was crooked, but not unfriendly. He held a small round ball in one of his hands. He was barefoot.

"You've only been here a little while," the man said. "Need some guidance?" He was speaking Pallastan, not radically different from Teutan, but with an odd inflection.

"I'm sure I do," Kiril said. "How long have you been here?"

"A year or two. Maybe three. I'm not sure. You're not from Weggismarche, but you speak the tongue pretty well—traveled far?"

Kiril nodded. "For a long time. From Mediweva, thousands of kilometers, tens of thousands."

"Not familiar with it. My name is Jury."

"Kiril." They shook hands.

"This place will take getting used to. So will the secret. You found the secret yet?"

"No. Is it the ball?"

"No," the ball said in a child's voice. Kiril started back, then caught himself and pretended to be stepping to pick up his pack. The Pallastan smiled.

"Not strictly the secret," he said, "but it'll help you understand. I don't listen to it much anymore. You have to ask it a question before it'll answer, except maybe when you first see it. Then it'll tell you what it is."

"Do we all get them?"

"You learn fast. You must know about the migration, then."

Kiril nodded. "What are they?"

"They say they're part of the world. That's their spiel. I don't trust them anymore, not completely. Keep mine around," he hefted it, "because it knows a few useful things."

"Where do I find mine?"

Jury pointed at the spot in the wall where Kiril had entered the dome. "Back through there. There's a place where we get food and water and a place to sleep, if you want to use it."

"Then let's go."

"Your woman die, too?" Jury asked, hesitating before the faintly luminous circle.

"She didn't die. She turned solid, like ice or silver."

"As good as dead. Mine did that. Legend told me what to do—or rather my father told what to do. He died of old age just before I left. I felt obligated to follow through. But now that I'm here—well, it's another story."

"I've got pretty strong reasons."

"You came a long way. Saw lots of strange things, too, I'll bet."

Kiril nodded. Jury motioned for him to step through first.

They stood in a square-cornered hall. At the end of the hall was a large circular room with a domed ceiling. A bright, warm bulge in the ceiling provided light and heat. Parts of the floor were spongy. There was a table in the center of the room, austere and white. As they approached, the table hummed and bowls appeared. They were uncovered and some steamed. The smell was appetizing. Two contained a thick, souplike fluid. Others held fruit and raw vegetables. "Thank you," Jury said to the walls. He picked up a cup of cold red liquid and toasted Kiril, then squatted on his haunches to eat and drink.

"Yours," he said. He moved a bowl with some effort—it seemed weighted to the table, or magnetized, and could not be lifted off—and showed him another ball. Kiril picked it up. "Well, go ahead," Jury prompted. "Ask it something."

He dropped it into his baggy shirt pocket. "I'll wait until later."

Jury shrugged and dipped his fingers into the soup, licking them off. "No utensils," he said. "Make you eat like beasts."

When they had eaten their fill they moved back from the table. The bowls vanished, merging with the table top. "There's another place you'll want to see sometime between now and sleep. After a while you'll get used to the sequence of places to go around here. You use the same door, but you go a different place each time. First there's the observatory—the glass dome we just came from—then you go here, then to the next place." He dropped a fruit core onto the table top. It liquified and was absorbed. "But you never go back to the tunnel in the Wall. Won't let you."

"I'm ready," Kiril said. He stood and wiped his hands on his pants, but saw he didn't need to. They were clean. Jury walked ahead of him and slipped through the circle. He followed.

They stepped into a glass-walled, cramped cabin no longer on the Wall's upper surface or anywhere inside. The entry circle was mounted on a slab in the middle of the cabin and opened onto a direct view of the lands below the Wall. They could see the wall's edge and the glowing columns along the edge that performed the same function as the Obelisks.

Walking around the slab, which was only a few centimeters thick, they looked beyond the rim of the world they had known. That way lay darkness, relieved only by the infrequent fire doves. Kiril looked down. And down. The Wall ended. Beyond was a river of night. Vaguely sinuous, the strip of black meandered between the grayness of the Wall's surface and another surface beyond. The two Walls, back to back, were at least three thousand kilometers wide. To either side they vanished into gentle curves. He recalled Bar-Woten's figure on Hegira's size—249,000 kilometers broad. He did a quick calculation in his head—780,000 kilometers in circumference.

Beyond the river of night and the second Wall was another landscape. It looked different, as if seen through a red glass and distorted. That, Kiril guessed, was the home of the thin ones.

He felt dizzy.

"No need to worry," Jury said. "If you'll look below, out that way, you'll see we're on an arch. It's holding us up. We're not flying or anything silly."

"What's that beyond the river, the black strip?"

"Another section of Hegira. Something like ours, I'm not sure how different. What do you think?"

"I'd like to know what Hegira is," Kiril said.

"Ask the ball," Jury said. "It'll tell you, but you won't understand. It doesn't know how to talk to mere humans, mere Second-born."

"How much will I understand?"

"Depends on what you learned before you got here. If you're one of them crazy people just below the Wall you might understand a lot. But I haven't seen any of them come through here—guess they're getting cut off for some reason. If you come from someplace like Pallasta, you might understand a little. You might spend years trying, like me, anyway, and get some idea. I understand a bit—not nearly enough. I was only a road-crew worker."

The next section of Hegira was moving perceptibly with relation to them, spinning opposite the section that contained the world he knew. "What's under us?" he asked.

"Please specify," the ball in his pocket requested. The childlike voice still surprised him.

"What's in the darkness between the Walls?"

"A near vacuum. At the center of Hegira, beneath all the sections, lies a singularity."

"Ah," Jury sighed. "That's a hard one. It's going to take a while to explain that one."

"Then I'll ask later."

"Just as hard later."

"What is Hegira?" Kiril asked the ball.

"I'll answer that," Jury said.

"Misinformation is not allowed. This extension will answer."

"I can give it to him simply!" Jury protested.

"There can be no brief explanation," the child-voice said.

"Here, put that thing down for a minute—"

"Jury has not made a crossing," the sphere said calmly. "There can be no understanding without a crossing." Jury started to speak, but Kiril held up his hand angry and confused.

"Is my woman's doppelganger on the other side?" he asked.

"Yes."

"It's lying," Jury said with a sneer. "Your woman has no double out there, nor does mine."

"Incorrect."

"Put that thing down and come listen!" the Pallastan said sternly.

A portion of Bar-Woten still remained in Kiril, a tiny inner homunculus, which had a life and judgment of its own. It told him the Pallastan was not very reliable.

"I'll stick with the ball," Kiril said just as sternly. The Pallastan took a deep breath.

"I've got no reason to cross," he said. "The Obelisk wiped out my country. My woman couldn't have survived that, no matter what state she was in."

"Did you ask the ball?"

"No," he said. "I don't want to know. You're a damned sight more inquisitive than I am. All right, do as you please. Do whatever you want. Ask it anything. You'll end up just like the others—you'll go through the tube and never be seen again! Go ahead!" Jury smiled broadly, but his hands trembled. He went through the circle, and Kiril was alone.

"Tell me what Hegira is," he demanded a moment later.

"It will take a long time," the sphere said. "It will involve a history of the First-born."

"I'm ready," Kiril said. Two others inside—at least two—also waited.

There was no immediate mystery or mystic beauty, only a child's voice letting him know this was business for cerebral absorption, and not religious inspiration. Generations after could look back on the story with awe if they wished—for now, it had to be explained coldly and rationally.

The voice was distant, as if heard through a broad stretch of cave, but without echoes. Its intonations were not precisely human. No human larynx had put the words together, only an approximation; and no human mind had structured their order or the sense behind them. Kiril detected a weariness behind what was said, not physical, or even spiritual—he didn't know how to describe it. It was as though the medium that carried the sound of the words was itself incredibly old and tired. The effect was one of falling dust and enclosing darkness. He began to shiver uncontrollably. Pictures came to his mind that couldn't have been conjured by words alone.

He didn't understand it all. Some of it was hideously alien to him. But he listened anyway.

25

"I have built this world called Flight," the voice began, "have designed it and arranged for its construction, have populated it with beings of all kinds, and have started again the process of action and event, that these creatures might think and exist as living things did long ago.

"The time has come for all the people of Hegira to know why they are called Second-born. You are no less than the First-born, but serve a different purpose. You are descendants and seed, and your life is the agony of an egg.

"The First-born had no such support and comfort as you might find now. They worked and loved and suffered very hard, as hard as any other species, to achieve what they achieved; and it wasn't a bad job.

"The Obelisks tell their story to the end of their existence as physical beings. Soon the Second-born will read more and be more prepared to come here and listen. But for the moment I will tell you in a way you might understand.

"From a condition not much different from yours on old Earth, the First-born worked and built until they could send ships far out to the planets around their star called the Sun. They populated the planets where possible, then sent ships out to other stars. At first the journeys were slow, but knowledge increased and old laws bowed to new refinements. Ships soon traveled very fast and shot through the clouds of stars in days and weeks and months instead of lifetimes.

"There were other intelligent beings beside humanity. Sometimes they met, and at first the meetings were confused, often destructive, always educational. Two thousand years of this made the First-born part of a very accomplished civilization, with cooperation from thousands of nonhuman intelligences. This civilization filled the whirlpool of three hundred billion stars, which the First-born called their galaxy.

"In this time the First-born came in a number of forms. Some humans changed themselves by adding machines to their bodies so they could live in places where they would otherwise die. Others grew used to deep space, far from the attractions of planets, and changed their shapes naturally and artificially. Still others, to live in the peculiar places where ships went to travel faster than a beam of light, adapted themselves to dimensions other than our own. Wars and disputes sometimes broke out between the different forms of the First-born, and between humanity and other beings, and between other beings and different forms of their own kind. It was a restless age.

"In time some species found it desirable to mingle their elements of life with those of the First-born, and inter-species breeding developed. The results were clumsy at first, and progress was difficult. But soon there were as many crossbred beings as there were individuals of distinct species. It was not a sexual communing in any usual sense—rather an exchange of strengths and a repression of weaknesses. All species benefited. To explain the ways of life these beings experienced is difficult—you have nothing to compare with them.

"Toward the end of the four thousand years the First-born began to understand their purpose. Their understanding wasn't the scattered hinting and searching of isolated philosophers—that sort of thing had been going on since before recorded history—but a deep-seated awareness that changed the way the First-born behaved.

"For centuries they had been in the path of a wind they hadn't even been aware of. The pressure of their calling, at the very moment of the diaspora, had almost reduced them to children. The tensions of the seed-expelling fibers had increased—young had become more prevalent, and with them their uncertainties, their sometimes violent frustrations and aggressions. The First-born had come to emulate, even worship, the bright, difficult young. In those easily unbalanced decades their lopped perspective came close to destroying them. They so often lost balance, swaying this way and that, but always the sway aimed them outward.

"They looked back and saw that on Earth they had been both muscle and seed. Like the mechanism of pods in a poppy flower, human intelligence and technology had resulted in muscular tensions building, then exploding. That explosion had carried the seed of Earth-life far into space. Human spirit, the First-born learned, was subservient to a higher force, which they had always thought was a lower one—the propagation of living forms.

"They discovered a genetic similarity between species, and that to reach higher stages of development a number of species would have to combine. They would then become a super-species—a new tool in the development of life.

"After this step it soon became obvious that nonliving things played a part in the life-history of the galaxy in much the same way the calcium of bones and dead proteins of hair and outer skin allow you to survive. The inorganic world was actually shaped by the organic world to its own purposes, through subtle forces and effects, which, again, are difficult to explain.

"But a few hints might give you the sense of it. There were natural extensions of living things into other universes, and these behaved according to laws as strict as any for the conscious world of the First-born. So-called ghosts, demons, and other influences were extensions of the living substance of most species and served definite purposes, either as repositories of racial memory or as protection from destructive forces—much like your dead outer skin protects you from damage. This interaction of states of life and death, at the end of the fourth millennium of the Space Age, gave a new clue to the progress and change of the First-born and their kin. Just as the migration of life from galaxy to galaxy began, the Space Age became subservient to another, far longer age— two billion years, the Age of Dissolution.

"It becomes even more difficult to explain. Some humans were still shaped much like yourself and thought in much the same way you do. There are backwaters in any development, especially when the development is rapid. But other species and superspecies were advancing to the point where a language using words cannot describe them. Poetry just begins by allowing vagueness. Mathematics can be a useful tool, but not in any form you now understand. Suffice it to say that organic and inorganic merged throughout hundreds of millions of galaxies. For a time those who had been left in the backwaters of change thought they lived in a dead universe, with only stars and rocky worlds left to explore. They could not see what was actually there—sooner that a bacterium in a man's gut could aspire to be the man.

"This organic nature of inorganic things revealed structures and superstructures of reality that could be changed. Metaphysics became as fluid a tool as physics. Realities were altered and tailored. The Age of Dissolution blended into a new period, which I cannot describe to you at all—the Unknown Span.

"To assign any length of time to the Unknown Span is inappropriate. It would be more appropriate to assign levels of energy and degrees of equations regarding basic entropic functions, which had not, and could not, be altered. The Unknown Span soon brushed against the inevitable, the death of the superorganism that the universe had always been, but was only now self-aware of. The subgroupings, which at one time had thought of themselves variously as superspecies, species, and individuals—all worked to continue the spread of life in the universe to come.

"All things are nested together, and between all things there must be commerce and exchange. Even so universes. In that Unknown Span, Hegira and the millions of sister-worlds, which you call fire doves were created. I am an extension of Hegira, which is itself aware.

"Hegira is a hollow shell made up of sections like the latitudinal slicings of an empty fruit rind. At the center of Hegira is a singularity, a black hole in space-time. This is a mass so dense that nothing can escape from the well of its gravitation. It is spinning, and when the inside of Hegira shoots bits of itself around the singularity, they return with even greater energy drawn from the spin, and this powers the world. You might think of an enormous top that spins only on the inside.

"Soon, in a few million years, Hegira's singularity will lose all of its rotational energy, and Hegira will die. Before that time you will build ships and leave for other worlds to start life again in the new universe.

"All of the worlds like Hegira together create a singularity with themselves inside. This universe-in-itself floats through the destruction of the old universe, already finished. Even now rents and distortions in the egg-universe begin. You have seen these as the nights with stars. When these distortions occur we take our bearings in the new universe and decide what you living things will have to face. The new universe is not exactly like the old.

"This was known long before the Unknown Span, that succeeding universes differ. You are therefore not exactly like the First-born. The small differences these changes made in the preparation of Hegira resulted in anomalies of animal and plant life.

"Second-born humans occupy this section of Hegira. Other intelligent species occupy the other sections. There has been some premature development and even intermingling ahead of schedule. You and your brothers are precocious."

Kiril sat on the floor of the cramped cabin and squeezed his head to quell a birthing headache. Then he stood and stretched his muscles, mulling over what had been said. He asked questions for hours and tried to understand the answers. Why there were only two children born to a woman; how long the Second-born had lived on Hegira; why all children were born with the ability to read the script of the Obelisks, but not the languages; what part animals played on Hegira; what Hegira was made of; and so on.

The ball answered in its weary child's voice whenever the answer could be given. And still he found most of it confusing. It was too much to absorb all at once. These matters of universes and singularities were clearly beyond him—someone else would have to think them through. No doubt they'd be discussed on the Obelisks.

Now that he was faced with the answer, he couldn't accept it. All of the humanity and history and existence he had ever known had to be more than a single seed shot with thousands of others in a diaspora.

He took a deep breath and picked up the ball from the floor. Then he went into the circle, and the tower vanished.

"Where am I?" he asked.

"The tube," the ball answered simply. "If you walk to the end you will be taken across the gap to the other section."

"What'll I find there?"

"You must cross to discover."

"What if that isn't good enough? What if I don't cross?"

"Then you'll end up like Jury. But you've come too far to stop now."

He looked down the length of the cavernous tube. It was ringed every ten paces by a protruding black band, and a red pathway showed him where to walk.

It seemed to stretch off to infinity. Behind him it went back as far, uninterrupted except for the slab that held the entry circle.

"You told Jury all that too."

"He hesitated. It's better not to hesitate."

He didn't like being told these things by a child. "I suppose my woman's double is across there."

"In a manner of speaking." That wasn't as definite as he wished. He held back. But unlike Jury he had to act for two others. And he had to act for Elena, though he could hardly remember what she looked like. She was a pain in the back of his mind, and he realized any chance to eliminate that pain was more than welcome.

"Why was I chosen?"

The ball didn't answer. Kiril waited, then asked again. "Why was I chosen? Why not somebody else?"

"You would not understand the answer."

He laughed. "I don't understand much of anything else, either. Try me."

"Put simply, because you had a better chance to survive. Because you would not go insane. You will return and carry your knowledge, and it will not kill you, at least not as it might kill others. Humans are very delicate."

"I think you skipped the most important part of the story," Kiril said. "You jumped over, I don't know how many, countless trillions of lives—people living and dying and being happy and sad—especially sad— maybe most of them were miserable. You skipped all that. It's like looking down an endless road, and there are these scattered bones lying piled on all sides, and they were our fathers and mothers and grandparents and so on, all leading up to you and your builders—

and to me. They've been forgotten like so many corals in a reef."

Again the ball was quiet for a moment. Then it said: "I don't think anything has been forgotten. Those who built Hegira had to go back to reclaim what time had lost. They found more than the texts of Obelisks and Walls. They found all you say was forgotten."

"Then what about us? Millions of people killed by falling Obelisks, more killed trying to reach the Wall . . . driving us like ants in a nest . . . couldn't there be a better way?"

"There was no better way. Pain and disaster are necessary elements in your life."

Kiril tried to say something more several times, but what he had to say seemed no more coherent than the cry of a child.

"There is more," the ball said. "Those who built Hegira no longer exist. The weight of the past hung on them just as entropy hung on the dying universe. Even had time been endless they would have required a final forgetting. They knew what you speak about. They knew the pressure of time's unavoidable evil. Do not be self-righteous. They knew far better than you."

There was nothing more to say.

He started to walk.

It took only a few moments. There was a blurring of his vision. After rubbing his eyes he found he could see a slab blocking the tube a few hundred meters ahead of him. He followed the red path and stepped through the circle.

26

Jury lay on the floor, asleep. Kiril stepped on him and nearly fell over. The Pallastan sat up quickly and got to his knees. "Careful, there!" he said. He stood and brushed himself off.

"I thought you weren't going to cross."

"You shamed me into it. I got sick of just sponging off the table back there. Besides," he said, "I asked the ball if my woman was alive. It said there was no way she could be killed. But it might take me a while to find her."

The chamber was so vast its far edge seemed lost. The roof was claustrophobically low, only a few centimeters above their heads. The wall was divided into phone-booth-size partitions, all of which were covered by transparent doors. All appeared empty.

The air smelled of medicine.

The floor was covered by a thin, spongy substance that deadened their footsteps.

Kiril took the ball from his pocket. "What do we do now?" he asked it.

"Find the booth that has a light in it," it answered. "Since Jury is with you, there will be two, together."

"I don't see it," Jury said, turning around.

"Follow the perimeter until you do."

It took them six hours. When they found the paired booths, both filled with a milky, opaque glow, they peered in and saw nothing. But before they could ask another question the glows began to take shape. Sparks and rainbows were whittled away until the boxes held two young men. One looked like the young scrittori who had fallen and killed himself on Obelisk Tara, in Mediweva, so long ago. The other was familiar to Jury. The figures faded and vanished.

"Wait!" Kiril screamed, pounding on the glass. Jury stood limply and tittered, holding two fingers over his mouth. Then he broke into laughter.

"You've found them," the ball said. "Now you can return home."

"But we have to take them with us," Kiril protested, his voice hoarse.

"No need. They are both dead. There can be no bringing back now. All you have to do is return with what you saw here. In fact," and it seemed to speak through a smile, "your women are already free of their affliction and have been since you entered the tube."

"Then we go back," Jury said to Kiril. "My woman will be half out of her mind, she wakes up and everybody's dead and the cities are gone. If she doesn't wake up buried someplace," he amended.

"She is alive," the ball assured him.

"How do we get back?" Kiril asked.

"Find the circle."

Whether it was the same circle they had come from or another some distance across the chamber, they never knew. They stepped into it a few seconds apart and never saw each other again.

Kiril woke from a sound night's sleep on a hillside

in a country he barely recognized, clothed but un-
shod, and without his ball. He was found by a sheriff
a day later walking west on a narrow dirt cart road,
taken to a local deputato, and arrested for vagrancy.
It took him three weeks to prove who he was. He was
released into the hands of a visiting church cleric who
recognized him. The dough-cheeked, acne-scarred
cleric lent him an ass, and together, poor and humble,
they trekked across a thousand kilometers of Mediweva, stopping at villages and inns of varying repute.
Nothing seemed to have changed much. The knowledge of the north hadn't reached Mediweva yet.

Obelisk Tara, the southernmost of the two in Mediweva, was a guide and beacon for them. After a
month of travel, interrupted by visits to the churches
of local dioceses for conferences—the cleric's business—they came to the village where Kiril had been
raised. There they parted company. Kiril shook the
hooded man's hand. "Go with God," he told him.

Then he went to the house of Elena's family. It was
empty except for a thin, tired-looking servant.

"They're at their ranch for the summer," the servant
said. "They're celebrating a miracle and a wedding."

"A wedding?"

"Yes! The Lady Elena has been restored to health,
and she is to wed a fine prelate."

That, said one of the homunculi inside of him, will
not do at all.

"Where will this wedding be?"

The servant hesitantly told him, butting a broom
handle nervously on the floor. "Don't I know you?" he
asked.

"Yes," Kiril said. "We met some time ago, before
Elena—" He cut himself off. "No time to waste!"

There was a bank account he had never touched, a small one that held the funds he had been given for his scrittori apprenticeship. He was glad he hadn't turned it over to the Brotherhood of Francis. He proved his identity by signature and code, retrieved his funds, and bought passage on a steam wagon.

He left the steam wagon near the gate to the ranch and walked unobserved to the stone house. He stood by a window south of the porch, peeping inside through the thin lace curtains on tiptoe atop the log planking that surrounded the house. He could see inside well enough, but there was no sign of Elena. He frowned fiercely, impatiently, and lowered his head as someone passed near the window. He recognized some of the people in the sitting room. One of them was Lisbeth, Elena's godmother, a slow, dull woman, earthy and direct. She was talking to a man whose face he didn't recognize. Her expression was more animated than usual. The man looked sleepy; Kiril knew the lassitude one could fall into listening to Lisbeth.

There was also, behind the couple and near the corner desk, a boy, Elena's youngest brother, who was working string figures on his fingers. He looked very much like the doppelganger whose death had begun the long journey ages ago.

Kiril circled around the house, keeping a close lookout for anyone who might see him. Anger was building in him at the thought that a simple church prelate—a godly man, probably, pious and inexperienced and kind—might have already sampled what he had gone to the end of the world to save. His face reddened. Not even the memory of distant Golumbine, where the reverse had happened, could calm him. In fact it stung him to further resolve. He had given up more than time to reach this goal! He'd given up sanity in love and the basic sort of satisfaction he might have had, had he stayed in Mediweva, contented in his life and work. Now that he knew what the world was about, and what was to come, he had to build solid foundations as quickly as possible, for himself and for others. Otherwise, he feared, they might all go mad.

He stood by the front porch and took a deep breath. No more eavesdropping. He would be direct. The sky was already darkening. In an hour or so the fire doves would be out, and if he didn't act before then the steam cart would leave and strand him until the morning. He had to move quickly.

He knocked heavily on the wooden door. Endless seconds later a servant answered, and thankfully didn't recognize him. He said he was a good friend of the family, and he'd like to speak to the father on important business matters.

"The master is busy at the moment," the tall, weary-eyed old man said. "Eating dinner and having guests. May I announce you?"

"No," Kiril said, breaking past and stomping through the anteroom and hallway. "No time!"

The family had just finished the evening meal and sat before a large fire in the tall, wood-walled living room. Elena was sitting at the knees of a man he knew instantly was the prelate. Kiril stood in the broad entranceway for a breath or two, all eyes turning to examine him. Elena's eyes, most important of all, went wide, and she choked in her cup of wine.

"I've come," he said, knowing it was melodramatic, and pausing for emphasis, "come for what is mine." It was a grand, stomach-churning moment. His armpits were lakes. His forehead was slick. His tongue was sure and unfaltering.

"Alfred Karl!" the father shouted at the butler. "Who let this man in unannounced?"

"I let myself in. Elena, come here."

The father and mother then recognized him.

"I will not be stopped!" Kiril said, holding up a toughened hand. He was sleek and muscular beneath his soiled white clothes, and well tanned, an altogether different sort compared to the pale, scholarly fellow who had wooed, mourned, and then vanished over two years before. "I've gone through hell for you," he told Elena. She didn't look quite as he remembered her. She wasn't quite as radiant. "Besides, I'm an important man now. Extremely important." Yes, he told himself, quivering. But would anyone believe that? If his voice was firm enough.

"Kiril, I can't leave now," Elena said, her face dampening with tears. "Something has happened. . . ."

He walked across the room, over the woven rug in the center of the circle of family chairs and sofas, and reached down to take her arm. The prelate gaped and stood up, almost falling back over the chair as his legs flexed abruptly against the edge. "What are you doing?" he demanded. His voice, compared to Kiril's, was a small yap. Still, Kiril acknowledged, trying to be fair, he was not unhandsome, and his face did show some courage. He felt sorry for the man.

He reached down and took Elena's arm. Her wide, green, eyes were accusing, shocked, and—he thought—happy. Conquering and returning and changed for the better and all that, he fantasized. He lifted her off the floor. The prelate reached for him and seemed to magically miss, as if he were ungraspable, a ghost. But he was solid flesh, only more agile now.

"I can't go!" Elena wailed. "You can't take me back!"

"I can, and will, and you will not protest!" He hauled her into the night through the flailing arms of servants, parents, and prelate. She didn't protest much after they were outside. The steam wagon waited at the end of the road, beyond the gate and tall fir trees. He picked her up in his gnarled hands and put her in the cab. The cart moved off at his direction. People shouted in the road behind.

Elena, stiff as a board, sat in one corner of the cart and looked at him, shocked and scared. "Come on," he murmured, not looking at her. "I haven't been gone that long, not as far as you're concerned."

"They said you'd been gone for years while I was asleep."

"You weren't asleep," Kiril said firmly.

She suddenly went limp like a doll, sobbing. Then, just as quickly, she wailed, "Where have you been?" and hit his shoulder with several stinging slaps. "Where in God's name have you been?"

"I'm a determined man now," Kiril said. But he still felt like a young boy in places. His assurance didn't run through him unflawed.

The wagon stopped abruptly, and the coachman swung down from his seat, cursing and praying loudly. The illumination of the night outside had changed. It was brighter. Kiril took Elena from the coach and showed her the stars in the sky and the wisps of glow between.

"See all this?" he asked. "I know what it is. I'll explain it to you soon." Then he ordered the coachman to drive on and told her they'd better get used to things that way.

The stars were there to stay.